THE FORGOTTEN ROAD

RICHARD PAUL EVANS

LARGE PRINT PRESS
A part of Gale, a Cengage Company

Farmington Hills, Mich • San Francisco • New York • Waterville, Maine
Meriden, Conn • Mason, Ohio • Chicago

Copyright © 2018 by Richard Paul Evans.
Large Print Press, a part of Gale, a Cengage Company.

ALL RIGHTS RESERVED
This book is a work of fiction. Any references to historical events, real people, or real places are used fictitiously. Other names, characters, places, and events are products of the author's imagination, and any resemblance to actual events or locales or persons, living or dead, is entirely coincidental.
The text of this Large Print edition is unabridged.
Other aspects of the book may vary from the original edition.
Set in 16 pt. Plantin.

LIBRARY OF CONGRESS CIP DATA ON FILE.
CATALOGUING IN PUBLICATION FOR THIS BOOK
IS AVAILABLE FROM THE LIBRARY OF CONGRESS.

ISBN-13: 978-1-4328-4552-0 (hardcover)
ISBN-13: 978-1-4328-4567-4 (paperback)

Published in 2019 by arrangement with Simon & Schuster, Inc.

Printed in the United States of America
1 2 3 4 5 6 7 23 22 21 20 19

CUNARD

❖❖

Library

Out of respect for your fellow guests, please return all books as soon as possible. We would also request that books are not taken off the ship as they can easily be damaged by the sun, sea and sand.

Please ensure that books are returned the day before you disembark, failure to do so will incur a charge to your on board account, the same will happen to any damaged books.

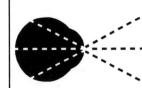

This Large Print Book carries the
Seal of Approval of N.A.V.H.

and crew on board were killed. What they didn't know — what no one knew — was that there were only 211 passengers on board.

As stated flatteringly in my obituary, I was a seminar presenter. A stage salesman. I sold the Charles James Wealth package. In older days I would have been called a huckster or charlatan — the successor of a snake-oil salesman. It's a prestigious line, really, attached to famous names like Rasputin and Charles Ponzi.

Working the stage, I railed at people who believed in fate. "Fate," I taught, "is the refuge of losers who don't take responsibility for their lives." Professionally, I had to take this position. People who believe in fate don't buy high-priced wealth packages to change their future.

Yet here I was, as swept away by circumstances as a swimmer pulled over Niagara Falls.

Was fate the reason I was still alive? If so, why would it choose me to survive? Maybe fate has a sense of humor.

One thing I was certain of was that I couldn't stay in my house much longer. People would be coming. People always come together after a death. I wondered how it would happen. In most cases of death there are spouses and partners, mourning family, all connected to the deceased, coming together to complete the tasks and rituals of death.

That wouldn't happen with me. My mother and brother were likely still alive, but I hadn't heard from either of them for more than a decade. The only familial obligation I had was a legal one. It was the child support payment I made monthly to Monica. I suppose that would be the first in a long series of legal actions.

I couldn't stay in the house, but I wasn't ready to leave Chicago either. As I lay in bed thinking about where to go, I heard a noise downstairs. Someone was opening my door. Someone with a key.

My heart froze. *Already?* I walked out of my room and peered around the corner to see who it was.

The door swung open. At first no one entered. Then a woman hobbled in sideways, awkwardly dragging two large suitcases. It was Marta, one of my cleaning ladies. She was a fairly recent addition to the crew. She spoke no English and mostly kept to herself. Now she had come to take my things. My first thought was to go charging downstairs, but I stopped myself. Was it

worth losing my anonymity over a few knickknacks?

Still, the thought of her stealing from me infuriated me. I felt as though I was living the fourth stave of *A Christmas Carol,* where people invade Scrooge's home to claim his belongings, stealing the very shirt from his body. "Why wasn't he natural in his lifetime? If he had been, he'd have had somebody to look after him when he was struck with Death . . ."

As I thought the situation through, I realized that I had nothing to lose in confronting her. First, who was she going to tell? She was new to America and didn't speak English. She could tell her boss, but since she had no business being in my house alone, she would likely be fired. Second, even if she somehow did tell someone, who would believe her? I was dead. Dead as a coffin nail. It was her word against the overwhelming crush of media.

I quietly walked downstairs to the dining room, where Marta was putting a silver serving platter into one of her bags. That platter had been a Christmas gift from Amanda two years back. I waited until she finished, then said, *"Hola, Marta. Qué tal?"*

I don't know if Marta's horror came from being caught stealing, seeing a ghost, or —

19

the worst possible scenario — being caught stealing from a ghost, but no matter; she was out of my house like an Olympic sprinter off the starting blocks, leaving her loot and suitcases behind. Honestly, I didn't know she could move that fast. I wouldn't have guessed it from watching her clean my house.

Back to my dilemma. As underscored by Marta's appearance, the fact was, I couldn't remain in my house. I needed a place to stay while I prepared for my journey.

Fortunately, there were several hotels within walking distance, including one I'd put a client up in just three blocks from my home. The Write Inn. I called and made a reservation.

Next, to plan for my walk. My hiking equipment was kept in my garage in a storage bin that probably hadn't been opened since I'd filled it. For someone who never hiked, I had premium equipment — expensive and never used. I had purchased the bulk of it when I was dating a swimsuit model who liked to hike. We broke up before I had even taken the tags off the equipment.

The first thing I retrieved from the locker was a backpack. All I knew about the pack was that the guy at the sporting goods store

said it was one of the best ever made — and their most expensive. Bizarrely, the second reason was more important than the first. I always bought the most expensive version of everything I purchased. Always. There was something deeply psychological about this habit. I bought the best of everything not necessarily because I wanted it — there were actually times that I would have preferred another option. I bought the best *because I could.* I suppose that's what happens when you grow up with deprivation. You feel driven to purchase what you would have been denied before, just to prove that you can't be denied now.

I filled my pack with only the most essential things: a water bottle, a rain tarp, a sleeping bag and inflatable pad, a one-man tent, and a small first-aid kit.

In spite of my lack of camping experience, packing for the road wasn't especially daunting. I'd been living on the road for months at a time, and it's not like I was heading to Nepal or hiking K2. What I didn't have I could always purchase. And since I would be carrying it all, I wanted everything to be as minimal as possible.

I carried the pack back to my room, then emptied my travel hygiene kit, sorted through what I needed, and put it all in a small, waterproof bag, along with a bottle of hand sanitizer and a tub of Clorox disinfectant wipes. So much for my OCD.

I filled the rest of the pack with clothing. I figured I would need more socks than usual. I packed rain gear, underwear, two pairs of light pants, and some basketball shorts. All softer fabrics and blends, nothing that would chafe. It was one of the few times in my recent life that I didn't pack a tie.

I also packed a pair of sunglasses and one of those crushable wool felt fedoras that made me look like Indiana Jones.

I went into my walk-in closet and pushed my suits to the side, revealing a wall safe. I took out a vinyl bank bag that contained the ten thousand dollars that I kept for emergencies. I don't know what kind of emergency would require 10k in cash, but it just seemed like a good idea. It was also where I kept my handgun, a 9 mm Smith & Wesson, along with a box containing fifty rounds of ammo. I was probably the only one in my neighborhood with a gun. Or at least the only one who would admit it.

I took out the Rolex watch my partners had given me in Las Vegas a few years back. It was an 18-karat gold President Day-Date with a diamond face. It retailed for more than fifty thousand dollars. The partners had given it to me to celebrate the milestone of the Charles James Wealth Seminars reaching a half-billion dollars in sales. It was the last time we met. We broke up the company three months later.

Of course, a Rolex isn't the kind of watch one would usually take on a cross-country walking trip, but it wasn't something one would just leave behind either.

In the back of the safe was something that had sat undisturbed since I put it in there seven years before. I reached in and pulled out a small black velvet jewelry box. It was of greater worth than the Rolex, not in price but in personal value. It felt almost like a religious relic. It was Monica's wedding ring. I snapped open the box, revealing a white gold band with a seawater pearl surrounded by marquise-cut diamonds. A pearl flower. It was the ring I'd given to Monica when I asked her to marry me. I smiled as I remembered the look on her face as I gave it to her.

My joy turned to pain as I remembered the look on her face as she took it off and set it on the stool behind the stage of the MGM Grand in Las Vegas. The moment was frozen in time, like a car crash. Her words, spoken softly, still echoed as loudly as shredding steel: "I'm not your pearl." I had thrown away my pearl of great price.

I unhooked the gold chain I wore around my neck and attached the ring to it. I was walking to her. It was fitting that I kept it close to my heart.

I went back to my nightstand and grabbed my leather journal. I was ultra-disciplined about writing in my journal. In fact, throughout my life I had filled twenty-three journals, which I stored in a private indoor storage site only Amanda knew about.

I grabbed my phone, this time remembering my charger, and carried my pack downstairs.

I locked the front door that Marta had opened and went to the kitchen. I opened the fridge and drank some milk directly from the carton, then poured the rest down the sink. I didn't know when, or even if, I would ever come back, but if I did, I didn't want to return to one-hundred-day-old milk.

I slung the backpack over my shoulder and took a deep breath, taking in the moment. As I looked around, I felt a faint sentimentality toward the place. I had lived here for seven years, longer than any place else except for my childhood home. I had left that home because it was killing me. I left this one because I was dead.

As I opened the back door, I softly spoke my mantra. "There is no God but me."

I locked the door and walked to the end of the yard, where I had climbed over the fence the night before. I looked over the fence. There was only a single oncoming car. I waited until it passed, then lowered my pack over the fence and climbed over.

I opened my pack and brought out my hat and sunglasses. The hat sprang back into shape. The sunglasses I brought were the same ones I wore at seminars when I didn't want to be recognized. They were black, wraparound, military-grade Wiley X — the same kind Bradley Cooper wore in the movie *American Sniper.*

I lifted my backpack and walked west toward the hotel.

I hoped to avoid my neighbors — not that they would recognize me anyway. In the past seven years, I had only spoken to a few of them and that wasn't at any great length. I was on the road more than eight months out of the year, and when I was home it was usually after dark.

Oak Park is a quiet bedroom community about ten miles west of Chicago. My home was just off North Oak Park Avenue on Erie Street, just a block south of Ernest Hemingway's childhood home. I also lived less than a mile from Frank Lloyd Wright's home and studio. His influence was profound in the area, as he had designed more than twenty-five structures in Oak Park. It's where he perfected his signature prairie style architecture that changed not only the Oak Park landscape but the very course of twentieth-century architecture.

I felt conspicuous walking through the neighborhood with a backpack, but the sidewalks and asphalt were still puddled from the recent storm and my neighbors seemed content to stay inside.

It took me just a little more than ten minutes to reach the hotel. The Write Inn is a four-story, redbrick structure with a large green awning shadowing the front entrance. It is a boutique hotel, small by any standard, just sixty-five rooms.

As I walked into the hotel lobby, I saw a couple at the front counter. I walked up behind them to wait and was about to remove my sunglasses when the woman turned and looked at me. I knew her. I didn't remember how I knew her, but I did. She must have recognized me as well, or thought she did, as her gaze lingered longer than what is usually considered socially acceptable. With my hat and glasses on, I knew she couldn't have been certain. I casually looked away, pretending that I didn't notice her.

Then she turned back to the man and took his arm and they stepped away from the counter. I let go of the breath I hadn't realized I was holding. But then the couple stopped again and stood talking by the door.

The woman behind the desk looked up and asked, "May I help you?" She was close to my age, pale, with thick-rimmed, black-framed eyeglasses and curly black hair.

I shrugged off my pack and laid it up against a column, took out my wallet, then glanced over to see if the couple had left. They hadn't. "Just a moment," I said softly, acting as if I was trying to find my ID.

Then I remembered how I knew the woman. Kate. She had attended one of my seminars and had cornered me afterward. She had applied for a job as a presenter and was angry that I hadn't hired her. Crazy angry.

Kate had called me sexist in front of a crowd of clients. Amanda had spoken before I could. "Mr. James hires a lot of intelligent, talented women, which is precisely why you weren't hired." Kate had gone bright red, then turned and ran from the hall.

Kate glanced back over at me once more, and then they walked out of the hotel. I breathed out in relief.

"Yes," I said to the clerk, extracting my credit card from my wallet. "I'd like to check in." I handed her the card without speaking my name to draw less attention to it.

She briefly looked down at my credit card, then at her computer screen. "Mr. James. Welcome to the Write Inn. I have you in a king suite. You'll be staying for a week?"

"That's the plan."

"Just sign here," she said, handing me a form. "There's no smoking."

"That's not a problem."

"Will you be parking a car with us?"

"No." I initialed the form and handed it back.

She ran my keycards and put them in an envelope. "You're on the fourth floor. The elevator is around the corner. Do you need any help with your luggage?"

"No, thank you. I just have my pack."

"Have a nice stay."

I put the keycards in my pocket, lifted my pack, and walked to the open elevator. The fourth floor hallway was partially barricaded by housekeeping carts, and I had to take off my pack to get through.

Once inside the privacy of my room, I leaned my pack against the wall and removed my sunglasses. The room's design was surprisingly dated. It had brass candelabra light fixtures, pale-yellow walls with camel-colored upholstered armchairs and dark blue carpet. The bed had a high, colonial-style mahogany headboard with a gaudy red-and-gold paisley duvet. It looked like they were trying to keep the décor authentic to Hemingway's era.

As I lay back on the bed, someone knocked on my door. My chest froze, revealing to myself my anxiety. What was I so nervous about? Maybe it was because I was using a dead man's credit card.

I walked to the door and looked out the peephole. It was only a cleaning woman, her arms piled with towels. I opened the door.

"Excuse me, sir," she said with a thick Russian accent. "I did not leave towels. May I come in?"

"Please."

I stepped back and she hurried into the bathroom, returning a few seconds later. "Thank you, sir. Have a good day."

"You too." I held the door for her as she hurried out.

Besides a swig of milk, I hadn't had anything to eat. My favorite Vietnamese restaurant was only two blocks away, but eating there was out of the question. The hotel's restaurant was called Hemmingway's Bistro, noticeably spelled with two *m*s instead of one, probably to avoid licensing fees or a lawsuit.

I sat down on the bed to look over the room service menu. I ordered French onion soup and a chicken Waldorf salad with a glass of red wine. Then I turned on the television to the local news. They were still talking about Flight 227. O'Hare handles more flights per day than any other airport in North America except for Hartsfield–Jackson in Atlanta, and the talking heads were giving updates on the crash as well as the subsequent chaos in the country's air travel, showing video after video of stranded travelers bedding down in airports across America. When room service brought my lunch, I turned off the news to eat in silence.

I spent the rest of the afternoon studying and charting my route. Route 66 is said to be 2,448 miles long, but actually, with all its different alignments and multiple roads, there is no exact number. The Route crosses eight states and three time zones, beginning in Chicago and ending in Santa Monica, California — where my Monica was. Where I had once been happy. Maybe, the last time I was truly happy.

I didn't know how long it would take to walk the Route, since I really had no idea how many miles a day I could walk. Using my smartphone and a notepad, I planned out my walk as far as St. Louis, Missouri, which is where I had last seen McKay, and where he'd told me he was dying.

I worked on my plans straight through dinner and called down to order a beet arugula salad, a half dozen Blue Point oysters on the shell, and chilled lobster.

Then I put away my notes and retired to the television to catch the NBA playoffs, which, unfortunately, the Chicago Bulls wouldn't be participating in this year. I had been too distracted to follow the playoffs, so I didn't know what teams would be playing tonight. It turned out to be the Atlanta Hawks and the Cleveland Cavaliers. *Cleveland.* There were two teams in the NBA that I loved — the Chicago Bulls and whoever was playing Cleveland.

I have nothing against the city of Cleveland itself. I love Cleveland. The people are friendly, it's the home of the Rock & Roll Hall of Fame, the Velvet Tango room, Drew Carey, and Calvin and Hobbes. Some of my biggest sales had come from the city. But it was LeBron James and the Cleveland Cavaliers who had knocked the Bulls out of the playoffs last year. Then, to add rock-sized salt to the wound, media pundits had the audacity of comparing LeBron James to Michael Jordan, which, to us Chicagoans, was as sacrilegious as John Lennon comparing the Beatles to Jesus Christ.

The Cavaliers crushed the Hawks by more than twenty points.

Chapter Two

Survivor's Guilt Is a Peculiar Thing. Why Would Our Psyche Torture Itself for Doing What It Was Primarily Designed For? — Charles James's Diary

THURSDAY, MAY 5

I woke the next morning to the room spinning. I felt nauseous and dizzy — seasick without a drop of ocean in sight. I crawled out of bed to the toilet and threw up. Twice.

I had felt this dizzy only once before. It was two years ago. I was in North Carolina and I had a big show in Dearborn, Michigan, I couldn't miss. I threw up once on the plane, twice in the Detroit airport, and two more times backstage — just two minutes before going on stage.

Amanda had gotten me some medicine that helped but I didn't remember what it was or even if I had needed a prescription.

Amanda and I had that kind of relationship. She'd hand me a document and I'd sign it without reading it. She'd hand me pills and I'd swallow them without asking what they were. I knew she would take care of me. I just wished that I had her here to take care of me now.

I dialed the front desk and was greeted by an overly cheery voice.

"Good afternoon, Mr. James. How may I help you?"

"Does the hotel have a concierge?"

"Yes, I can help you. What can I do for you?"

"I'm not feeling well. I need someone to pick up something for me. I need something for dizziness. I don't know what, something over-the-counter."

"There's a Walgreens a couple blocks from the hotel. I'll see what I can find. Can I get you anything else?"

"Maybe some Gatorade. And ice. Lots of ice. I could use an ice pack."

"Yes, sir. Something for dizziness, Gatorade, ice, and an ice pack. Give me about a half hour."

"Thank you," I said, and hung up. I went to the bathroom and wet a washcloth with cold water, put it over my face, and went back to bed. As I lay there I wondered how

34

much of what I was feeling was psychosomatic. Or was it just a coincidence that my life was spinning out of control and now my head was as well?

I hated the thought. Part of my stage shtick was my mantra, "Take control of your mind, take control of your life." Here I was, completely bereft of control of both. Then again, maybe there was a simple explanation. Like a brain tumor.

It seemed like hours before the hotel guy knocked on my door — a young man with red hair and bushy red eyebrows. He was holding a Walgreens sack in one hand and a hotel ice bucket in the other. A rolled newspaper was wedged under his arm. "May I come in?" he asked.

"Please."

He walked to the table and set down the ice bucket and sack, laid out the newspaper, and then proceeded to hold up the items for me to see.

"The pharmacist recommended Bonine for dizziness. Here's your Gatorade and your ice pack. I also brought a copy of today's paper. I thought you probably wouldn't be going out."

"Thank you."

"Shall I put this on your bill?"

"Yes, please."

"Very good. Is there anything else I can do for you?"

"Wait. Just a minute." I went to my pack and pulled out a twenty-dollar bill. "Here. Thanks for your help."

"My pleasure, sir. I hope you feel better."

"Thank you. Me too."

After he left, I washed down two Bonine tablets with half the bottle of Gatorade, then went back to bed. As I lay there, not only was the room spinning, my thoughts were as well. What-ifs were bouncing around in my head like numbered balls in a bingo cage. So many things could have changed Tuesday's outcome. Stupid things. *What if* I had not stopped at the office for the birthday celebration? *What if* the flight attendant had reopened the Jetway door for me? *What if* the obnoxious clerk at the shop hadn't been so slow? Everything that had annoyed me at the time had collaborated to save my life.

Of course, my what-ifs were the foundation of a much bigger question swirling around in my head. *Why was I still alive?* Of 211 people, there must have been at least one life worthier of saving than mine. Maybe all of them.

I realized that what I was feeling was survivor's guilt. I wanted to talk to my therapist, Christine Fordham, and get her take on all this. I picked up my phone and began looking for her number, then stopped myself. I couldn't do that anymore. *I was dead.* I wondered if therapists were bound to the same confidentiality standards as lawyers, that she couldn't disclose anything about me. Or, when it came to legal consequences, was she required to report me? I could see it going either way.

A half hour later my dizziness had eased some, so I gingerly got up and googled *survivor's guilt* on my smartphone. A slew of entries came up. The first thing to catch my eye was a story about country singer Waylon Jennings. It turns out that wailing Waylon and I had something in common. We had both barely missed dying in a plane crash.

Jennings was supposed to be on the infamous flight carrying Buddy Holly, Ritchie Valens, and J. P. "The Big Bopper" Richardson. Jennings was a guitarist for Buddy Holly's band and had a seat on the plane but, at the last moment, had given up his seat to Richardson because the Big Bopper was ill and didn't think he could take the long bus ride. (Another guitarist in Holly's band, Tommy Allsup, was also supposed to be on that flight but lost his seat to Ritchie

Valens on a coin toss.)

Just before getting on the plane, Buddy Holly said to Jennings, "I hope your ol' bus freezes up." Jennings replied, "Well, Holly, I hope your ol' plane crashes."

It was the last thing Jennings said to the legend. The article said that Jennings suffered the rest of his life with survivor's guilt. *Not helpful,* I thought. At least I hadn't told anyone that I hoped their plane crashed.

The next article I read was clinical: "The Cause and Treatment of Survivor's Guilt." The article offered the following advice.

1. Recognize that your feelings are a normal reaction to abnormal circumstances.
2. Share your feelings with a friend or family member.
3. Take time to mourn.
4. Turn your feelings into action.

Step one wasn't difficult. My circumstances were about as abnormal as they could be. Two wasn't going to happen. Three, I would have more than enough time to mourn. And four, positive or not, walking Route 66 was definitely a lot of action.

I went back to bed and didn't wake until the next morning.

CHAPTER THREE

**MAYBE IT'S BETTER TO GO
THROUGH LIFE WITH OUR
SELF-DECEITS HIDDEN BENEATH A
ROCK THAN TO LIFT THE STONE AND
WATCH THEM WRITHE IN THE LIGHT.
— CHARLES JAMES'S DIARY**

FRIDAY, MAY 6

I woke feeling a lot better. I still felt as if I had been run over by a truck, but at least the truck wasn't parked on my head.

After throwing up most of the previous day, I was famished. My stomach was still a little upset, so I ordered a large stack of pancakes from room service, along with a Coke to settle my stomach. Then I went back to planning my walk.

I'd left off at the eastern outskirts of St. Louis, which were a bit confusing. St. Louis had diced Route 66 into so many pieces that it was difficult to know where to go. I finally just figured that it really didn't matter which road I took, since just about every road west had, at one time, been part of the Route.

St. Louis was about sixty-five miles east of the Meramec Caverns. This was significant for me. The caverns were a known hideout of my great-great-grandfather Jesse James. Cave explorers had found both his signature and a bank box from one of the trains he robbed. I felt as if I was going to visit a family shrine.

Then I noticed the newspaper that the hotel employee had left in my room the day before. I picked it up and began scanning the headlines.

City Tries New Tactic for Museum
Students Write to Slain Classmate
For GOP a New Reality Sinks In
15-Year-Old Missing South Side Girl
Found Safe
Families Mourn Victims of
O'Hare Plane Crash

Families mourn. I turned to the article printed next to the obituaries, which, because of the crash, were several pages longer than usual.

I read the article. Then, as I fanned through the obit pages, something caught my eye. It was a picture of me posted above my obituary.

In a way, reading about my life was even more surreal than reading about my death — the whole of my existence summarized in a few short paragraphs. That was it. My legacy.

When I was in eighth grade, my English teacher had given us the assignment of writing our own obituary. As macabre as it sounds, the point of the exercise was to force us to examine our own existence. That's exactly what I was doing now. There were things I would have liked to have added to my obituary. "A loving husband and father" would have been nice.

At the end of the article was an invitation to my memorial service.

There will be a cocktail party, memorial reception in Charles's honor at the Crystal Gardens Navy Pier, Sunday, May 8, from noon to three. In lieu of flowers, please send a donation to The Christmas Box International (Utah) to help abused and neglected children.

A cocktail party at Crystal Gardens. I had no doubt that the service had been planned by Amanda. She had taken care of me in life. Now she was taking care of me in death. The Crystal Gardens venue would not be cheap, but at least she was spending my money on me.

As I read over the obituary, an idea lit my mind. *What if I attended my own memorial service?* Isn't that what everyone fantasizes about? And the Crystal Gardens was the kind of place I could pull it off. The Navy Pier was always crowded, but it would be even more so this Sunday because it was Mother's Day, making it easy to blend in with the masses.

Still, I would have to go incognito. There was some risk of being seen, but I doubted that anyone would recognize me. Mostly because they weren't looking for me. Half of recognition is expectation. Also, by then, I'd be four days in on growing my facial hair. Add to that my hat and dark glasses, I would be just another mourner in the crowd. I could attend my service, then start my walk.

My walk. Maybe it was the sudden excitement of thinking about my own service, but suddenly walking seemed like a bad idea. Wasn't there another way to look at things? Against all odds, my life was spared. This was a time to celebrate my life, not run from it. Didn't I have everything people wanted

— friends, fortune, celebrity? Why would anyone in their right mind walk away from all this? *That's the point,* I thought. I wasn't *in* my right mind. The last three months, with the weird dreams and drama, I had felt as though I had been taking crazy pills. But that's all it was, just a few bad months. A few bad months followed by a wildly traumatic experience.

Clearly, I was being rash — a victim of the turbulence of my life. Everything would be okay. I just needed to get back into the swing of things.

My memorial service would be the perfect place for my triumphant return. What a story. It would make national news. All the newspapers and morning shows. Especially considering how much press the plane crash had generated and was still generating. There wouldn't be another article that didn't include the story of the one survivor of 227.

I looked again at my obituary. I couldn't have created a better media buildup myself, and I was an expert at building hype. I was a showman. What better show could I give my fans than a return from the dead? I mean, it had been done once before, right? Two thousand years ago. People were still talking about that.

I could imagine it — hundreds, maybe thousands of people at my memorial service, everyone who knew me, everyone whose life I'd touched, all gathered together to mourn the demise of the great Charles James. Then, when Amanda got up to say something sweetly sentimental, I would walk up, take the microphone from her, remove my hat and glasses, and . . . what would my line be?

My mind reeled with possibilities. *You know what they say, it's hard to keep a good man down.* Or *What a landing, folks . . .* (Probably too soon for that one.) Or Twain's classic line, *Sorry, friends, but news of my death has been greatly exaggerated.* Or how about a line that had never before been spoken: *So glad you could all make it to my funeral.*

I smiled. No matter the line, the shock value was going to be off the charts. It's what we call in the seminar business an "epic reveal." That's exactly what Sunday was going to be — an epic reveal. Easily one of the most epic reveals of the year. Maybe one of the most epic reveals of all time.

Turns out it would be. But only for me.

CHAPTER FOUR

**I'M NOT JUST READY TO GET
BACK IN THE SADDLE — I'M READY
TO RIDE THIS THING TO THE
TRIPLE CROWN.
— CHARLES JAMES'S DIARY**

SATURDAY, MAY 7

Saturday was a blur, the calm before the squall. Emotionally, I felt the best I had in months. I was excited for the first time in a long time. I was going back a winner.

I spent the better part of the day looking over my calendar and planning my return, not just at my memorial service, but in life and business. I was ready to get back to work. I was ready to make, as I preached from the stage, *mega*-money. Private-jet, private-island money.

In my hiatus I had missed three shows in two cities. They could be rescheduled, but now with better press. Who wouldn't want to interview the man who cheated death? And I'd have a better stage story. A much better one. One that people would pay to hear.

For the last five years I had shared my "near-death" experience — an exaggeration about almost drowning on Flamands Beach in Saint Barts. My new story blew that one out of the water, pun intended.

I would start my machine back up in Denver. I had lost hundreds of thousands of dollars, but if we spun this right, we could make that up and then some in one show with all the added media.

My notes and plans for my trip across Route 66 sat abandoned on the hotel table. I had already moved on. The idea for the trip had been a detour — a distraction until the real plan unfolded itself.

After the sun set, I ate a celebratory dinner of escargot, prime rib, and a bottle of 2007 Corison's cabernet. Then, under the cover of night, I walked back to my home and retrieved a suit, dress shoes, shirt, and tie. My nicest.

I was tempted to just sleep at my house and pick my stuff up from the hotel in the morning. It really didn't matter whether anyone saw me. By Monday I would be back among the living, continuing where I had left off.

In the end, I decided to go back to the hotel, mostly out of convenience. I hung the suit up in the closet and went back to working on my speech. Tomorrow would be one of the greatest days of my life.

Chapter Five

I Once Read That Unrequited Love Is Never Lost — Rather, the Universe Returns It to Us. I Don't Think Mine Came with the Boomerang Effect.
— Charles James's Diary

SUNDAY, MAY 8 (MOTHER'S DAY)

Mother's Day was always complex for me. It had started at a young age. Amid the mass dysfunction of my childhood, there was one incident that stood out. When I was in the fourth grade, in Mrs. Drake's class, Mother's Day was a big production. Usually elementary school teachers would have their kids make something kitschy for their mothers, like a gold spray-painted macaroni necklace or a handprint in plaster, but Mrs. Drake was a professional potter. She helped us make heirlooms.

Several weeks before Mother's Day, Mrs.

Drake brought in a block of clay and gave us each a slice. Following her instructions, we sculpted little plates and tea cups, carving our names in the bottom with toothpicks. Then she took our crooked little tea sets home and glazed and fired them. We were all excited when they came back, hard and shiny. But we weren't done. We still got to decorate them.

We wrote HAPPY MOTHER'S DAY in the center of the plates, then we painted around them. I painted my plate with flowers (my mother loved flowers) and then put two big hearts on the teacup. Then I painted little hearts around the rim of my cup with a vine running between them connecting them. I was proud of my work, especially when Mrs. Drake held up my cup to show the rest of the class.

Then Mrs. Drake took our creations and again glazed and fired them. When we got them back, they were magnificent. Michelangelo could not have been more proud of his *David* than we were of those cups and saucers. I couldn't wait to give my mother her gift.

That next Sunday, Mother's Day, my little brother gave my mother a hand-drawn card and an unwrapped Reese's peanut butter cup. I remember looking at his feeble offering and feeling vastly superior to him.

Then I presented my tea set. I had put it in a shoe box. My mother carefully lifted it out and looked at it. She smiled at me and said, "Thank you, Charles. It's beautiful."

I beamed. I had pleased her.

Two days later my father told me to empty all the garbage cans. As I poured the plastic garbage can from my parents' bathroom into the outdoor trash can, my cup and saucer fell out. I reached into the trash and lifted the cup out. My mother didn't want it. It was a stupid present. I was stupid to think she would like it.

I threw the cup in the street, listening to it shatter into a hundred pieces on the asphalt. It wasn't just that *it* wasn't good enough for her. I knew that *I* wasn't good enough for her. That night my father beat me for not taking out all the garbage. It wasn't nearly as painful as how I felt about my mother's rejection.

I spent most of my life trying to earn my mother's love before I learned that love can't be earned. Earned love isn't love; it's an emotional wage, a paycheck for time served.

I was fully twenty years old before I learned that. My wife, Monica, was my teacher. She cared, unconditionally, for that broken little boy in me.

Several years before I blew up our marriage, Monica and I had talked about having children. She always said, "I hope I have a little boy who looks just like you." She got her boy but lost me. I had completely failed another mother.

For a brief, insane moment, I thought of calling Monica, but I convinced myself that that was a bad idea on many levels. First, she no doubt thought I was dead. Second, I hoped she would be at my memorial. And third, there was the possibility that she might be happy that I was dead.

With all that in my head, I got ready for my memorial service.

It felt good to dress up again. I looked nice in my suit. I should: it was an Ermenegildo Zegna and cost nearly thirty grand. Then I put on my hat and sunglasses. With that and my newly sprouted facial hair I hardly recognized myself.

I got an Uber for my ride into town. The driver arrived promptly and dropped me off on Grand Ave. As I expected, the pier was teeming with people. I put on my hat and sunglasses and got out of the car. I casually looked around to see if I recognized anyone. I wondered how many of those around me had come to pay their respects.

Navy Pier was originally designed to be a commercial dock for freight and passenger boats with additional space for public recreation. Since then it had had a mercurial history. As commercial docking declined or moved to other ports, alternative uses were proposed for the space.

Then, in 1989, the City of Chicago created the Metropolitan Pier and Exposition Authority to oversee the property. Five years later the Navy Pier was opened to the public as a waterfront promenade featuring restaurants, shopping, and world-class entertainment along with the Crystal Gardens, a one-acre, indoor botanical garden designed for weddings, receptions, and corporate events. The Garden's pavilion is an impressive six-story atrium with a fifty-foot arched ceiling above more than eighty palm trees.

The revitalization succeeded and today the Pier is Chicago's number one tourist attraction. The Pier, along with the Crystal Gardens, were familiar to me. My company had reserved the venue for several of my wealth seminars as well as a few other functions.

The Crystal Gardens are located near the front of the pier, and as I walked toward the building, I passed a woman selling roses from a kiosk. I stopped and bought a dozen red roses, just in case Monica was there. It would be my first Mother's Day present for her and an interesting twist, since she might have brought flowers for me. Bouquet in hand, I got on the escalator and stepped off on the second floor into a large, open lobby leading into the gardens.

I had expected to encounter a crowd upstairs but the room was nearly vacant. I wondered if I'd gotten the wrong time or day, so I took the obituary out of my pocket and checked the information. It was the right place, day, and hour. It was five minutes to noon.

There was a chrome, free-standing event sign near the front doors that read in forty-point type:

Charles James Gonzales
Memorial Service

Where was everyone? There was no security by the door, just a bored-looking young woman I'd never seen before with long blond hair and a dark-navy velvet dress sitting on a folding chair. She had a small stack of programs in her lap and what looked like a full box of them on the ground next to her. She was engrossed in her smart-phone.

I walked up to her. "Excuse me. Could I have one of those?"

She looked up from her phone and grabbed a program from her lap. "Sure. Here you go."

"Thank you," I said. "Hand out a lot of these today?"

"No. Like six, maybe."

I stepped past her into the massive atrium. The room was warm and humid and the muted tones of organ music echoed throughout the space. The Crystal Gardens atrium can hold more than a thousand people and it appeared that Amanda had optimistically booked the whole of it for my service. From what I could see, she could have fit everyone in the coat closet.

There were hundreds of white slipcovered chairs tied with satin bows fanning out before an oak lectern adorned with an elegant funeral spray of white roses, chrysanthemums, and Asiatic lilies. Next to the lectern were two colorful, medium-sized bouquets of flowers and a pinkish-orange carnation and gladiolus wreath on a three-legged stand. In front of the flowers, on an easel, was a picture of me.

I glanced down at my watch. It was now

one minute to noon. If this were one of my seminars, I'd be apoplectic by now. As it was, I was speechless.

There were fewer than a dozen people inside, not including the catering staff. Tuxedo-clad waiters with wingtip shirts and black band ties roamed the space carrying trays of hors d'oeuvres. There were more servers than guests.

I found myself nervously looking for Monica. Had she come? Had she been invited? The only person I recognized from my distance was Amanda, who was, in her usual way, bouncing from place to place, making sure that everything was going as planned.

One of the waiters spotted me and decided to make the trip. When he got to me, he held out a tray with cracked crab claws.

"Would you like some crab, sir?" he asked.

"Yes. Thank you." I took three portions. I might as well. I was paying for it. "Thank you," I said again.

"Don't mention it. Here, take more," he said, pushing his platter toward me. "It looks like there's going to be a ton of food left over."

I shook my head. "No thanks, I'm good."

He turned and walked back toward the kitchen.

I sat down on the very back row of chairs,

setting the bouquet of flowers on the seat next to me. I took a bite of crab, then looked down at the folded program the girl had handed me. The front of the program was a picture of me — a glamour shot I'd just had taken for my new tour and the same picture the newspaper had used with my obituary.

The information about me printed inside the program was pretty much a rerun of my obituary. On the inside right-hand page was an outline of a short, organized program conducted by Amanda.

I looked back toward the front of the room, where what there was of a gathering had now settled into the chairs. Amanda sat down in the front row between her secretary, Laura, and Stephen, my company's CFO. That was it from my office. Apparently the rest of my two dozen staff had something better to do. This piqued my anger. I planned to remind them of their absence when they asked for their jobs back.

And no Monica.

Seated next to Amanda's group was an older gentleman whom I didn't recognize — a tall, bald man wearing a light-blue suit with a navy or black scarf. To his side was a beautiful younger woman with long, strawberry-blond hair. There were two young boys next to her sitting remarkably still.

Then I realized that the man was McKay Benson. He had told me at our last meeting that he had cancer. He had lost his hair since then. But more surprising than his physical appearance was that he had flown with his family all the way from Florida to be here. The man whose business I had stolen, whose life I had upended, had come to my memorial service. He was far more of a class act than I had given him credit for. I suppose that's not surprising. We tend to demonize those we inflict pain on. It lessens our guilt.

Amanda glanced back down at her watch. Then she smoothed her hair, stood, and walked up to the lectern. She softly tapped the microphone, then leaned forward toward it. "Is this working? Can you hear me?" Amanda hated speaking in microphones. Actually, she hated all public speaking, which is why she stayed safely behind the curtain at all of our events.

McKay gave her a thumbs-up.

"I guess we'll get started." She looked around the vacant room, then all the way back at me. "Sir, you're welcome to join us up front."

I slightly panicked at being noticed. I just

raised my hand to imply I was good where I sat.

Amanda continued. "Thank you, everyone, for coming. I thought there would be a lot more people here, but it is Mother's Day."

Nice spin, I thought.

She looked down at the lectern. She had typed her eulogy.

"We are here today to honor a remarkable man. A good man, a good boss, and most of all, a good friend. No one could say that Charles James Gonzales didn't leave his mark on this world. Still, I think that he was sometimes misunderstood.

"Some people thought he was uncaring, because he was so demanding. But that's precisely why he was demanding, because he cared about us enough to not let us fail. Failure was never an option for him. And his success wasn't just for *him,* it was for all of us. It was for the team.

"I probably knew him better than anyone in this world." She hesitated, then reached for a tissue and dabbed her eyes. "I trusted him implicitly. I trusted him with my career. I trusted him with my time. I trusted him with my dreams. I always knew that he had my back. I miss him." She paused again. "Charles, if you're here today in spirit, I miss you, my dear friend." She wiped her eyes again, then walked back to her seat. She blew her nose. McKay reached over and patted her on the back.

I was moved by the sincerity of her emotion. I wiped my own eyes with a napkin that smelled of crab.

Next McKay stood. He was a little unsteady on his feet, and his wife handed him his cane. Then he placed on his head a wool Ivy Cap. He had always liked caps, and he looked good in them. He was one of those rare men who could pull them off.

He leaned on his cane as he walked to the lectern. Even as far back as I was, I could see that his health had deteriorated severely.

"Good afternoon," he said warmly to the small group, taking the time to make eye contact with each of them. "We have come here today to memorialize the life of a very special man, Charles James Gonzales. By way of disclosure, Charles and I didn't always see eye to eye." He smiled. "But geniuses rarely do."

There was a slight chuckle.

"I liked Charles from the moment I met him. Charles was a team player. He believed in making others look good, not just himself. He knew his job and he took it seriously.

"And he was a master on the stage. I

would watch him and my chest would swell with both pride and envy. Sometimes I felt like Salieri watching Mozart, simultaneously worshipping and envying him, but always admiring him. Charles had more natural talent and drive than any man I hired before or after him. I take pride in being the one who discovered him." McKay lifted a handkerchief and wiped his eyes.

"It's no secret that things didn't go well with us in the end. Our relationship ended in a lawsuit. There were some bad days and bad blood. There were bad words. Harsh words. But it wasn't all him. I played as big a part in our business divorce as he did. But I can honestly say that after the gavel came down and it was all over, what bothered me the most wasn't the lost business or the lost income, it was the loss of a friend.

"I want you to know something. Even though there were problems between us, I've never regretted giving Charles a chance or bringing him into the fold. Never.

"I don't fault him for his choices. In many ways he was as much a victim of them as anyone else. Charles was driven because he had to be. What made him great was also what made him volatile. He had grown up Dumpster-diving with his father, running from poverty. No, I don't fault him for wanting more.

"I had the opportunity to have dinner with Charles in the past month. It was good to see him. I'm grateful that I had that chance to let him know that I had come to peace with our past. And to let him know that I had forgiven him. I only wish that I had asked him to forgive me for not making him feel safe enough to trust me. That was my failure as a boss. And as a friend." McKay hesitated again. He again lifted the handkerchief and wiped his eyes. "Sorry, I didn't plan on being so emotional."

He wiped his eyes once more, then said, "You know, as I look back over my career, I can honestly say that the years I spent on the road with Charles were among the best of my life. Charles was like a son. Of course, that can be a mixed bag too."

Everyone chuckled.

"But that's how I thought of him. As the son I never had." He turned and smiled at the two boys in the front row. "Until these fine young men came along." His gaze lingered on them a moment before he looked back up. "I guess that's why our disagreements hurt so much."

Disagreements? I had betrayed him.

"Like you, Amanda, I also miss my friend." He forced a sad smile. "But unlike you, Amanda, it won't be for long. It won't be long before I'm pushing back the curtain on that big stage in the sky." He hesitated and I could feel the power of the emotion in the room. "I just hope that when I get there, I find Charles holding a microphone and mesmerizing an audience of angels. And I hope there's Scotch in heaven. Good Scotch. We'll have a drink for old times."

Even from the back of the room I could hear sniffling.

"You know, I do have one regret. I wish that Charles were around to watch my boys grow up. I think they would have liked him, just like I did. Thank you."

McKay grabbed his cane and limped back to his seat. Amanda and his wife both stood. Amanda hugged him. His wife did as well, then helped him sit.

Amanda walked back up to the lectern. "Is there anyone else who would like to share?"

No one moved. Then Amanda's secretary, Laura, raised her hand, stood, and walked up to the microphone. Amanda took a few steps back.

"Hi."

There was a small chorus of "Hi" back.

"I didn't know Mr. James very well. I was kind of afraid of him, but I liked to hear him talk. He was the best storyteller I've ever known. He was also the best salesman I've ever known. I swear he could sell a refrigerator to an Eskimo."

Laughter.

"I also knew that Amanda, my boss . . ." She turned back toward Amanda. "I knew that she really thought the world of him, so I knew that even though he could be scary . . . he was a really good guy. Thank you."

Scary?

Laura walked back to her chair and Amanda stepped back up to the lectern. "Thank you, Laura. Is there anyone else who would like to say anything?" She looked at me, raising her voice as she spoke. "Sir, would you like to share anything?"

I shook my head.

"Okay. Then that will conclude our service. Thank you, everyone, for coming. There's a lot of food, so please take a few boxes home with you. I won't have enough space in my car for it all."

I stood and hurried out of the room before anyone could see me, leaving my flowers on the chair where I'd set them. So much for my epic reveal.

CHAPTER SIX

**IT WOULD APPEAR THAT THE
GREATEST DUPE PRODUCED FROM
THE MILLIONS OF DOLLARS I'VE
SPENT IN HYPE IS MYSELF.
— CHARLES JAMES'S DIARY**

I stumbled out of the hall in a daze. I hailed a cab on Grand and headed back to Oak Park.

"Welcome back, sir," the clerk said as I walked into the hotel. "Glad to see you're feeling better."

I grunted a thank-you as I walked by. When I got to my room, I looked at my program, then wadded it up and threw it away.

I remembered a story about Alfred Nobel. Nobel, founder of the Nobel Peace Prize and the inventor of dynamite, was falsely reported dead when a French newspaper confused him with his brother, Ludwig, who died in a French hospital.

The press lauded his passing, calling him the "merchant of death." Nobel became so distraught over his legacy that he decided to create the Nobel Peace Prize, celebrating those who "have conferred the greatest benefit on mankind."

That pathetic memorial service was my legacy — my Alfred Nobel moment. No one cared about me except Amanda and the man I'd betrayed. Everything that mattered to me I'd given up. I had no reason to stay where I was, physically or figuratively. I had nothing to go back to. Something had to change. Something inside. In the meantime, I was going on my walk.

CHAPTER SEVEN

**THE PROBLEM WITH SIN IS THAT, IF
YOU HAVE A CONSCIENCE, YOU PAY
WHETHER YOU'RE CAUGHT OR NOT.
— CHARLES JAMES'S DIARY**

I woke the next day feeling dark inside. For the first time since the plane crash, I truly felt dead. I ordered breakfast from room service, then showered and got dressed, finishing as my food arrived. I ate quickly and went to work. There were details I needed to clear up before I started my walk.

I pushed aside my breakfast dishes and laid out all the cash I had on the table. Ten thousand dollars from my home safe, the three thousand Amanda had given me at the airport for the temp company in Cincinnati, and seventeen dollars left from petty cash. Thirteen thousand and change. I did the math in my head. Route 66 was about 2,500 miles, so that came to about five dollars a mile. If I walked twenty miles a day, that would be 125 days, giving me about a hundred dollars a day to live on. Less than what I was used to living on, but doable.

The most pressing thing I had to do before hitting the road was figure out how to protect my money. I didn't know what my future held yet, but I wanted my portfolio secured no matter what. At last count I had accumulated a net worth of nearly eight million dollars, scattered throughout various accounts. A lot could happen to that in a hundred days.

I used my smartphone to pull up my investment portfolio. There were seven different accounts: three business, two personal, and two investment accounts. The Charles James business accounts were sitting on more than two hundred thousand dollars of operational capital. Transferring money out of these accounts would be noticed immediately. Stephens, my CFO, would think my account had been hacked and the funds stolen, but I had no choice. If I kept my money in its current accounts, it would eventually be frozen, if not confiscated. The question was, Where could I safely park my money until I returned?

As I looked over my portfolio, I remembered that one of my accounts wasn't listed.

I smiled. I'd found an easy, unexpected solution. Six years earlier, at my partner Chris Folger's insistence, I had opened an offshore banking account in the Cayman Islands. It was during a lunch in Palm Springs while I was complaining about how much I owed in taxes that he started telling me how best to evade them through offshore banking. He said the Caymans were the new Switzerland, but without all the scrutiny. Truthfully, I had no interest in Folger's tax scheme, as I had no desire to spend time in prison for tax evasion — or to worry for the rest of my life about the possibility. Still, for whatever reason (likely that he wanted me to be criminally complicit), Folger insisted that I open an account and kept after me until I did. I put $25,000 in it and had pretty much forgotten about it until now. Fortunately, I kept all my account numbers in a secured financial app on my smartphone. I looked up the Cayman Island account number and began transferring all my funds into it.

It was a little before noon when I completed the last of the transactions. I was satisfied that I was ready. It was time to begin my walk. I put on my hat and sunglasses and left the hotel.

Chapter Eight

" 'Begin at the Beginning,' the King Said, Very Gravely, 'And Go on till You Come to the End: Then Stop.' " Lewis Carroll — Charles James's Diary

The start of Route 66 is in downtown Chicago. I didn't get an Uber this time. I wasn't in a hurry, and I was now on a self-imposed budget. From now on I would travel by foot or public transportation.

The Green Line metro station was just a few blocks south of the hotel. The Green Line has the reputation of being the most dodgy of all the metro lines into the city. The cars are about what you'd expect to find in any public place, though with the added bouquet of weed and urine. As I got on the train, my OCD kicked in and I had to wipe down the entire seat before sitting.

I took the train to the Adams/Wabash station. As I got off, I stepped in a puddle of vomit. Fortunately, the ground was still wet from rain and I scuffed my feet along the sidewalk until my shoe was clean.

Historically, the beginning of Route 66 has changed multiple times, but the currently accepted start is beneath a heavily decaled Route 66 sign on Adams Street, just a half block west of the Art Institute of Chicago. I touched the sign pole, then started my walk.

I'd probably walked Adams dozens of times before, but this time it looked different. It felt different. Maybe things always look different when we leave them, like a lover. Or a battleground. (Sometimes those are one and the same.)

Chicago sidewalks are filthy. There's nothing profound about that. All sidewalks are filthy, that's what happens when a million people walk on you, but in Chicago the sidewalks look as if they were poured that way. There are galaxies of black spots on the dirty surface, chewing gum that has been ground into the cement and become as hard as the pavement.

Some cities, like Palm Springs or Beverly Hills, seemed to spontaneously sprout from rich soil, as full and fragrant as hibiscus. Not Chicago. Chicago is the gnarled, stout tree that pushed itself out from stone, surviving in spite of the harsh environment — or perhaps because of it. Even the train runs above ground instead of beneath it, as if the earth below the city were just too hard to penetrate.

As I walked, I thought of the Chinese proverb *A journey of a thousand miles begins with a single step.* Indeed. Just one foot in front of the other. The city towered around me in stark contrast to where I'd end up if I made it. *If.* There's a lot to that two-letter word. All journeys face gravity and though I chose not to think about them, there were things that could stop my trek. I had no idea if I was up to seeing this all the way through. I could get hurt or sick. I could be mugged. I could even die. Wouldn't that be ironic?

It was a bustling Monday noontide and the streets were crowded with people scurrying off to lunches and appointments like mice in a concrete maze. Ahead of me, a window cleaner rappelled down a building, dropping like a spider on its line. I walked west on Adams, the long, skyscraper-lined corridor stretching out before me like a teeming cement canyon. In the distance I could see the freedom of a blue horizon.

I continued on the road, crossing the bridge over the Chicago river. To my left, the Sears Tower stretched 110 stories high. I know, its new name is the Willis Building, but, like most Chicagoans, I still called it the Sears Tower. It's not our fault. If someone changes their name after thirty-six years, the old name sticks.

The Sears Tower is interesting in many regards, not the least of which is that its design was inspired by a cigarette ad. It was the tallest building in the world for twenty-five years, but those kinds of records are made to be broken. Man will always seek the next tower to heaven.

I kept reminding myself that I was dead, just in case I ran into someone I knew. Fortunately, people on the streets of Chicago don't look at each other as they walk. It's an unwritten rule.

About a mile into my walk, I stopped to eat breakfast at Lou Mitchell's. Maybe it was just me getting in the mood for the Route 66 experience, but Lou Mitchell's is the consummate Route 66 diner and perhaps the most famous one of all. The restaurant boasts that since their opening in 1923 they've broken enough eggs to wrap around the world twice. It's the kind of place that campaigning US presidents visit to demonstrate their affinity for the city.

A small crowd was congregated just inside

the doorway. A woman walked up to me carrying a heart-shaped woven basket full of Lou's signature offering: sugared doughnut holes and small boxes of Milk Duds.

I took a doughnut hole, not because I wanted one but because I didn't want to refuse her. She told me that there was a twenty- to thirty-minute wait for a table, but I could have a seat at the counter and eat, which I did. I ordered coffee, a fruit cup, and a Route 66 special, an apple and cheese omelet.

A few minutes after I ordered, the man on the stool next to me, a gray-haired man with glasses and a sports coat, laid his newspaper in the no man's land between us, next to the Tabasco sauce and salt and pepper shakers.

The front page of the newspaper was an image of firemen shooting massive streams of water on an airplane's burning fuselage. The headline read:

FRIGHT 227. WHAT WENT WRONG.

The waitress set down a cup of coffee in front of me. I poured some cream into it and turned to the man next to me. "Do you mind if I look at your paper?"

He glanced over. "No. Help yourself."

"Thank you."

He added, "Tragic, that crash."

"Horrific," I replied. I read quickly, hoping to find new information. According to the article, the plane's cockpit voice recorder had been found, but FAA officials had not yet released the cause of the crash pending a full investigation. Some experts suggested mechanical malfunction, citing the separation of one of the engines on takeoff. Witnesses to the disaster reported that the plane had pitched sharply to the right shortly before crashing just three hundred yards from the end of the runway.

Then something near the end of the article caught my eye.

> . . . notable passengers included Chicago alderman Susan Lisowski, real estate mogul Charles "Chuck" McHenry and best-selling author Charles James.

I turned back to the man. "Could I buy this off you?"

"You can keep it. I'm done with it."

"Thank you." I tore out the article with my name, folded it up, and put it in my pocket.

The man watched me out of the corner of his eye, then asked, "You know someone on that flight?"

I hesitated. "Yes," I said, looking ahead. "I did."

"Sorry," he said.

The waitress delivered my omelet with a side of hash browns. As I ate, I overheard a conversation in one of the booths behind me. From the volume of the conversation I suspected that at least one of the women had hearing loss.

"You remember Frances, from the Sandersons' Christmas party last year?"

"Which Frances?"

"How many Franceses do you know? Frances Laflin. From Lincoln Park."

"Was she the one who drank too much and started singing 'White Christmas'?"

"That's her. Her daughter was on that flight."

"The one that crashed?"

"Yes."

"Oh my."

"What makes it worse is that she and Frances had just gone the rounds and weren't speaking to each other."

"That's a shame. What were they fighting about?"

"She never said. Probably had something to do with that boy her girl was engaged to."

"What a shame. It will probably haunt her for the rest of her life."

"Poor boy; he lost his fiancée."

I wondered how many conversations were going on about me. Was there anyone who might be haunted about my death? A better question was, Was there anyone who wasn't on my payroll who would even care?

When I finished eating, I paid my bill with cash and, putting on my sunglasses, walked back out of the restaurant. I continued west on Adams.

According to my notes, I was about twenty miles from my first destination, the city of McCook, Illinois. I've always been a fast walker and my natural pace was a fifteen-minute mile. At that rate I could cover the distance in a little more than five hours. Of course that pace didn't allow for a pack and I would slow as the day wore on, but even six hours would put me in McCook before dark.

Leaving the shadow of the city was both a relief and a problem. It was a relief to be free from the noise and congestion and the risk of being recognized. It was a problem because I was entering a part of the city that was blighted and potentially danger-ous. I knew the risks. Last year Chicago's rise in homicides was so steep that it single-handedly raised the national homicide rate, which was otherwise falling. And I was carrying a good deal of cash.

My worry was in vain. I passed only one other person, a homeless man, who was too busy trying to create his nest to even notice me.

I soon discovered a problem I hadn't considered. I found it difficult to keep to the road. Much of Route 66 has been paved over and renamed so many times that it isn't uncommon to find a stretch of road carrying two different names.

Fortunately, Illinois has an active Route 66 Association that works to keep the memory of the road, even the road itself, alive and relevant by lining the Route with signs. Otherwise much of the Route would already be untraceable.

Around one p.m. I reached the town of Berwyn. Route 66 passes through the center of the town, so the main road was copiously marked with Route 66 signage.

I passed through the town, then turned right on Joliet Street, which led me out of the suburban area. For much of that stretch there was no sidewalk, and so most of the day I walked off the side of the road on weeds and gravel.

I reached McCook at around six, the city heralded by a Las Vegas–style sign:

Ⓦ Ⓔ Ⓛ Ⓒ Ⓞ Ⓜ Ⓔ

TO *Fabulous* MCCOOK, ILLINOIS

JEFFREY TOBOLSKI, MAYOR

Directly under the sign stood a giant fiberglass rooster.

I was already tired and glad to be back in civilization — and by civilization I meant in proximity to a Target and Walmart. I was tired *and* hungry. A mile into town I stopped at a Lone Star restaurant and ate a bowl of baked potato soup, a wedge salad, and their largest steak, a twenty-ounce porterhouse.

This time I paid with my credit card. I figured that I might as well use it while I could. It would likely take the banks a little while to learn of my death and shut down my card. With the charges, they would assume that my ID had been stolen, something they were used to.

I read somewhere that the most common victims of identity fraud are the dead. Identities of more than a half million deceased Americans are stolen each year. According to the report, it can take financial institutions upwards of six months to register death records, giving thieves plenty of time to rack up charges. And since the dead don't monitor their accounts, the thieves usually get away with it. Many of these thieves even file tax returns under the deceased's identities, collecting an estimated five billion dollars a year.

I finished eating, then walked across the parking lot to check out a massive Harley Davidson dealership. For years I had toyed with the idea of buying a Harley but just never got around to it.

I browsed the bikes a while, then walked down the road to a Holiday Inn Express.

I checked in, dropped my pack off in my room, and then walked to a nearby Walgreens to purchase foot powder, moleskin, and Epsom salt. I went back to my hotel, filled the tub with Epsom salt and steaming hot water, and soaked until I was ready for bed.

For as anxious as I had felt before starting the walk, the day had been surprisingly uncomplicated and head clearing. Maybe this journey would be easier than I anticipated.

Just weeks later I would laugh at that thought.

Chapter Nine

One Day Down, a Hundred to Go. Could It Be That the Chains of My Life Are Already Beginning to Stretch?
— Charles James's Diary

The next morning my legs were sore but not terribly. The salts had helped.

I stretched my hamstrings, then got out of bed and read through my travel notes. It was about twenty-one miles to the city of Joliet, my day's destination. I went downstairs for the hotel's complimentary breakfast before collecting my pack and heading out.

Joliet Road was easy to follow and clearly marked with Route 66 signs. After two miles I saw a brown road sign at a junction.

ROUTE 66, USE THE 55 UNTIL
EXIT 268 TO JOLIET

Highway 55 was easy walking with wide, paved shoulders.

Besides industrial warehouses and manufacturing, there was nothing interesting for miles except for Montana Charlie's flea market, with another large rooster. I'm not sure what it is about oversized fiberglass roosters and Route 66, but I had only been on the road for two days and it was already my second encounter with a massive fowl.

About fourteen miles into the day's walk I entered Romeoville, passing the Romeoville High School, Lewis University, and two miles after that, the wide, well-manicured lawn and the tall, razor wire–topped fences and guard towers of Stateville Prison.

On the road, surrounding the perimeter of the prison, were signs that read

DO NOT PICK UP HITCHHIKERS

Especially those wearing orange prison jumpsuits, I thought.

Suddenly the repeated pop of gunfire filled the air, which was a bit disconcerting until I saw that it was coming not from the prison but from a nearby outdoor gun range.

A little more than two and a half miles southeast of the prison was the Old Joliet

Prison, a limestone institution made famous by the notoriety of some its inmates, including the two men from what an older world had named the "crime of the century," Nathan Leopold and Richard Loeb. (Their crime was later dramatized in Alfred Hitchcock's adaptation of Patrick Hamilton's play *Rope.*)

But it was the prison's life in media that had made it iconic. The building has been immortalized in dozens of books, poems, songs, and movies. It is perhaps best known for the opening scene of the 1980 film *The Blues Brothers.* John Belushi's character, "Joliet" Jake, got his name from the prison. (His brother, Elwood, was named for Elwood, Illinois, the next town west on the Route.)

I reached the Joliet city limits at around four in the afternoon. In spite of its small-town feel, it's the third-largest city in Illinois, trailing only Aurora (by a little) and Chicago (by a lot). The traffic became more congested as I approached the downtown area and the downtown area approached rush hour.

Joliet is one of the rare big cities that still claims its roots in Route 66, and its most notable Route icon, outside of the prison, is the Rich & Creamy ice cream stand — a boxy, white-shingled building with a large ice cream cone–shaped sign on its roof that reads, "JOLIET Kicks Route 66." Also on the roof are fiberglass replicas of Jake and Elwood, posed in their signature dancing stances.

A few miles later I passed Dicks on 66 — an auto repair shop with vintage cars parked in its lot and two old cars on the roof.

Joliet has earned her share of notoriety. In addition to its famed prison, its Rialto Square Theater was a favorite hangout for crime legend Al Capone.

I turned left on Ruby and crossed a riveted blue metal bridge. There are five drawbridges in Joliet, though I only saw two of them. They were picturesque.

In the center of the town is the century-old Saint Joseph's, an ornate, two-spired Catholic church. At one time Joliet was considered a religious town, nicknamed "the City of Spires" because of its many houses of worship (122). Now it's better known for its casinos, the largest being Harrah's Hotel and Casino, located in the city center.

Near the resort is the Joliet Area Historical Museum. The building that houses the museum was once a Methodist church but is now a shrine to Route 66, the church's cross replaced by a massive neon Route 66 sign. I went inside the museum to check it out and was quickly engulfed by two employees, Elaine and Zack. Their enthusiasm for the road was palpable.

"Route 66 is America as it used to be," Elaine said, her energy approaching that of a TV evangelist. "It's the last thoroughfare to the American dream." Her eyes lit up. "You know, Sir Paul McCartney of the Beatles stood right where you're standing now. Right there," she said, pointing at my feet. "That very spot. He was driving Route 66. He was an Englishman and we get a lot of Europeans driving the Route."

Her companion, Zack, was no less passionate. "Let me tell you, the way to do the Route is with a menu, not a map," he said. "Oh my goodness, you eat your way through 66!"

"I'll do my best," I told him. I paid the seven-dollar admission fee and led myself on a short tour. There were other exhibits in the museum besides Route 66, but they seemed almost out of place, including a section that honored former Joliet resident and rocket scientist John Houbolt, the "unsung hero" of the Apollo program. *Unsung* was accurate. I'd certainly never heard of him. Houbolt was the aerospace engineer credited with designing the lunar orbit rendezvous and putting a man on the moon.

The man had his critics. One scientist said, "Houbolt has a scheme that has a fifty percent chance of getting a man to the moon and a one percent chance of getting him back."

He got the astronauts back. I've always sided with the doer more than the critic.

Before leaving the museum I stopped in its prodigious gift shop, which sold every conceivable stripe of Route 66 memorabilia, from pencils, puzzles, and Christmas ornaments to patches, 3-D viewers, and refrigerator magnets. There were books and maps — scores of them — and they were something I needed. I purchased a spiral-bound travel guide and a large folded paper map. Up till then I had been using my cell phone to chart my way, something I was growing increasingly nervous about.

Before I left, Zack insisted that I try the Route 66 "Route Beer." I purchased a cold bottle and walked the few blocks to Harrah's, where I booked a room for the night.

CHAPTER TEN

**TO UNDERSTAND THE WORLD
WE LIVE IN, WE MUST FIRST
UNDERSTAND THAT WE ARE NOT
SEVEN BILLION PEOPLE OCCUPYING
ONE WORLD — RATHER, WE ARE
SEVEN BILLION WORLDS OCCUPYING
ONE PLANET.
— CHARLES JAMES'S DIARY**

In spite of the distance — I'd walked about twenty-three miles the day before — I felt pretty good the next morning. I walked back onto the main thoroughfare of Ottawa to 53, then after about a mile, under the 80 overpass, continuing along IL 53 — a road that clearly wasn't made for pedestrians. Joliet was also once a center for the steel industry, and I passed several iron companies on the way out of town.

A little after one o'clock I entered the town of Wilmington. One of the famous

Route 66 landmarks, the Gemini Giant, towered above the street near the city entrance. The twenty-foot fiberglass man held a rocket next to the Launching Pad Drive-in, which was closed and for sale.

The town looked like an oasis in time. The main street was lined with older but well-preserved buildings, including the still-operational yellow-bricked Mar Theatre and Kaveneys Drug & Soda. Both looked as though they had just recently been plucked from the fifties. Kaveneys had an impressive reproduction of *A Sunday Afternoon on the Island of La Grande Jatte* by Georges Seurat painted on its exterior wall.

As I walked through town, a woman hailed me. "Good afternoon," she called out affably.

"Good afternoon," I replied cautiously.

"Where are you going?" She was middle-aged with heavily bleached hair. At first I worried that she recognized me, but then I realized she was just being sociable. Or bored.

"California," I said.

She looked puzzled. "California. *The* California?"

I wondered what other California she knew of. "Yes, the state. I'm walking Route 66."

"Oh," she said, nodding slightly. "We get a lot of people coming through town traveling Route 66. Not walking of course, but in cars. Sometimes older ones, like Corvettes, like they drove on the *Route 66* television show. Sometimes they're on motorcycles. But not many walking."

"I wouldn't imagine," I said.

"It's a long walk," she said.

"Yes, it is," I said.

"I met a man once. A few years back. He was walking the Route." She paused to take a deep breath, then added, "He had a goat."

"A goat?"

"A goat. And a wagon. The goat was his friend. He had the wagon for when the goat got tired."

"He pulled the goat?"

"That's what he told me."

"I'm goatless," I said.

"I can see that."

"And wagonless."

"Yes. But you don't need one. You haven't got a goat."

I couldn't imagine anyplace else to go with the conversation, so I said, "It's nice meeting you."

I had turned to go when she said, "You weren't planning on staying at the motel, were you?"

She said this with such gravity that I stopped. "I don't know; why?"

"I wouldn't stay there. They found a decomposed body in it last week. Best to keep going."

"Thanks for the warning." I walked away with an amused grin on my face.

I reached the Van Dam motel around two. It was near the Wilmington Dam. The sign outside read, "Best motel by a dam site."

In spite of the woman's warning, I checked in to the motel. After inspecting my room for decomposing bodies, I went across the street to Nelly's, another landmark eating place I'm sure Zack in Joliet would crow about. Outside the restaurant was a sign that read, "Home of the Best Dam" burgers, beef, dogs, onion rings, fresh-cut fries.

There were Route 66 signs all over the outside of the restaurant, along with vintage gasoline pumps and flags from around the world.

Inside, the walls and ceiling were covered with the signatures and scribblings from decades of visitors. Almost as soon as I entered, a waitress approached me. She had a name tag pinned to the breast of her creamsicle-orange blouse: Tina. Seating me at a table, she asked, "You from out of town?"

"Yes."

"Where you staying? Van Dam?"

"Yes, ma'am."

"You know they found a decomposed body there last week."

"I heard that."

She nodded, then said, "Stay away from the dam."

"The dam?"

"It's a drowning machine. We've had eighteen drownings on record. Two more this Memorial Day."

"I'll keep my distance," I said. I was beginning to feel like I'd walked into the opening scene of a horror movie.

I ordered the Chicago-style Italian beef with mozzarella cheese and a large salad, a Coke, and a strawberry milkshake, then walked back to the motel. I stayed away from the dam.

Chapter Eleven

More Has Been Sacrificed in
the Shadows for Us to Live
Safely in the Light than We
Know. Perhaps More than We
Want to Know.
— Charles James's Diary

Based on the motel's online reviews — one
and a half stars out of five (one guest wrote,
"I don't think the place has been cleaned
since the Great Depression") — I wasn't
expecting much other than a bed, a bath, a
low price tag, and maybe a decomposing
body, all of which I got (except the body).

I slept in the next morning, leaving my
room around ten. Nelly's was closed, so I
started off without breakfast, following 66
across the Kankakee River. I stopped at
what I thought was a bakery but was actually a *barkery,* a place that made dog treats.

Outside Wilmington, I passed a neighborhood full of houses peculiarly decorated with lawn ornaments, including a cardboard cutout of a Sasquatch. The road had a very narrow shoulder, so I did a lot of walking on the railroad tracks.

I reached the town of Braidwood and the Polk-a-Dot Drive In a little before noon. I had read about the drive-in in the Route 66 guidebook I'd purchased in Joliet. The outside of the restaurant was adorned with fiberglass statues of Elvis, Marilyn Monroe, James Dean, and Betty Boop.

According to the write-up, the restaurant started in a polka dot school bus and then, after years of success, moved to an actual brick-and-mortar building.

I stopped for lunch, ordering a pizza burger, mashed potatoes and gravy, and two lemonades. I don't know if it was my walking-induced hunger or the food itself, but everything tasted extra delicious.

I had gotten a late start, so I ate quickly and got back out on the road. My guidebook also said to look for the Braidwood Zoo — which consisted of metal folk art of an elephant, polar bear, giraffe, cow, and steer — but I didn't stop. One thing else I found peculiar: there were a lot of black POW-MIA flags flying beneath American flags.

Outside Braidwood the landscape turned

bare and flat. An hour later I reached the village of Godley. Curiously, the town's telephone poles were uniformly tilted at a forty-five-degree angle.

The next town I came to was Braceville, followed by the larger Gardner, with its whopping population of 1,500. Gardner had also made my Route 66 guidebook for a still-extant two-cell jailhouse that had been used in the thirties for hobos and vagrants who hopped off the train looking for work. The guidebook said that the townspeople felt better having them locked up at night. Next to the jail was a horse-drawn streetcar used as a diner on Route 66 from 1932 to 1939.

A few minutes' walk from the town center, I came across a humble memorial for someone I had never heard of yet might have saved the world. The Reverend Christian Christiansen (which might be the most perfect name ever for a preacher) was born in 1859 along the west coast of Norway and immigrated to the United States in 1880. He was ordained in 1888 and became a circuit-riding preacher between the Illinois towns of York and Gardner. The reverend was in his eighties when he came across an article in the *Chicago Tribune* that changed history.

The article reported that the Nazis had built an atomic weapon plant in Christiansen's hometown in Norway — a site chosen because of its access to the heavy water needed in the production of a nuclear weapon. Even though the Allies' intelligence was aware of the plant, they were unable to launch a strike against it as it was naturally protected by a mountain shelf, and the fjord was too shallow for a battleship to navigate.

As a child, Christiansen had hiked every inch of the terrain, and he remembered it as well as he would his own backyard. He contacted the editor of the local newspaper, who helped him reach the proper officials in the US Navy.

High-ranking military and intelligence officers descended on the small town of Gardner and listened to Christiansen as he laid out for them in precise detail the mountain terrain. The vital information was passed along to the British military, who organized a commando raid known as Operation Gunnerside. The raid was successful and stopped the Nazis from completing their atomic bomb, a development that, no doubt, would have changed the outcome of the war. The operation was also immortalized in the 1965 film *The Heroes of Telemark,* starring Kirk Douglas and Richard Harris, though no mention was ever made of Christiansen or the role he played.

The memorial for the man was little more than an oxidized bronze plaque about the size of a piece of letterhead: a humble memorial for the man who might have helped save Western civilization.

The thought of this bothered me. In my career I had honored myself and been honored, far more than this man had ever been. I had received more standing ovations, gifts, and accolades than this man could have dreamed of. And for what? Taking people's money?

That thought rattled around my mind for the next sixteen miles, where Route 66 jogged sharply north, up and over the freeway overpass. I followed the original road, with I-55 to my left and railroad tracks to the right, along a lengthy strip of barren landscape. Ten miles later I stopped for the day at the Classic Inn.

I ate spaghetti and meatballs at Pete's Restaurant and Pancake House, then went back to my room and collapsed into bed.

CHAPTER TWELVE

THE AUTHORITIES HAVE FINALLY CONCLUSIVELY DETERMINED THE CAUSE OF THE PLANE CRASH. I'M SURE THE 211 DEAD CAN NOW BREATHE A COLLECTIVE SIGH OF RELIEF.
— CHARLES JAMES'S DIARY

I headed off the next morning to the town of Dwight. The town wasn't hard to find as it was announced by a massive baby-blue water tower with its name emblazoned in twenty-foot-high letters.

I walked into Dwight on Highway 47, passing the Ambler-Becker gas station, an iconic Route 66 station and landmark, then stopped at the Dwight laundry, threw most of my clothes into the washer, and walked farther down the street to eat breakfast at the Old 66 Family Restaurant. I had coffee, biscuits, and the Denver omelet.

After breakfast I walked back to the laundromat, moved my clothes to the dryer, then walked to Berkot's grocery store, where I purchased jerky, Advil, hard caramels, water, and a copy of *Time* magazine. I walked back to the laundromat and read the magazine while I waited for my clothes to dry.

There was an article in *Time* on the Flight 227 plane crash with more definitive information about the investigation. The FAA had concluded that the crash was due to mechanical malfunction. As the jet was beginning to take off, one of the engines separated from its mounts, damaging the wing and severing the hydraulic lines that kept the wing locked in place. As the jet started to climb, the left wing stalled while the right wing continued to lift, rolling the jet sideways and causing the crash. I could only imagine the terror the passengers must have felt as the plane rolled.

The jet had just been refueled, and the resulting explosion and fire had incinerated everything. No human remains were found.

When the dryer buzzed, I gathered up my clothes and went back on the road, leaving the magazine on top of the dryer.

The rural landscape was flat, littered with old barns, cornfields, and railroad tracks.

The road signs for 66 were now painted shields on the highway, the change likely made because Route tourists kept stealing the regular road signs for souvenirs.

I walked along a narrow, two-lane highway for another three miles until I reached the town of Odell. The town greeted me with four Burma-Shave-style signs placed in twenty-yard intervals:

A SMALL TOWN
WITH A BIG HEART
WHERE EVERYBODY
IS SOMEBODY

Near the entrance of the town was Odell's Standard Oil Gasoline Station — another vintage Route 66 filling station that had been restored by the people of Odell and the National Park Service. The station's design was based on the 1916 Standard Oil model known as the "domestic style" gas station, which looked more like a domicile than a place to fuel up. The idea was to leave the customers with a comfortable feeling they could associate with home. I had nothing on the marketing men of those days.

The Route then crossed through a small suburban area without a car in sight. My most surprising find was the Odell Subway

Tunnel, a pedestrian tunnel that went under the road, for schoolchildren and pedestrians who needed to cross the busy 66.

It was hard to imagine that the traffic through this sleepy suburb had once been so brisk that an underground crossing was needed. The tunnel has since been filled, so only the entry way and a few steps leading down still exist.

As I left the town, I encountered more Burma-Shave-style signs:

GOOD-BYE
GLAD YOU CAME
HEADED TO PONTIAC?
BE SURE TO VISIT
ROUTE 66 HALL OF FAME MUSEUM

They're working that rhyme like a rented mule, I thought.

Sixteen miles into my day's journey I encountered the first advertisement for the famous Meramec Caverns, painted on the side of a barn. Barnside advertising had once been a thing — before myriad billboards began cluttering our thoroughfares. Then the laws changed, and now only existing advertising barns are allowed to remain.

At about twenty miles, entering the town of Pontiac, I walked past the Old Log Cabin

Inn. My guidebook said that the restaurant actually predated Route 66 and its proprietors had turned the whole building around to face Route 66 after it was built.

I came upon still more Burma-Shave-style signage.

IF HUGGING
IS YOUR SPORT
TRADE IN YOUR CAR
FOR A DAVENPORT
BURMA-SHAVE

WHEN YOU
TRY TO PASS
THE GUY IN FRONT
GOES TWICE AS FAST
BURMA-SHAVE

From 1926 to 1963, the Burma-Shave company created hundreds of these advertising ditties (more than six hundred by one count), many of them becoming part of the American lexicon. Sometimes on our morning Dumpster dives, my father would recite one of his favorites, with as much gusto as if he were reciting Shelley or Whitman.

DRINKING DRIVERS
NOTHING WORSE

THEY PUT THE QUART
BEFORE THE HEARSE

One of the Burma-Shave signs even became a popular song of today.

HEY I JUST MET YOU
AND THIS IS CRAZY
BUT HERE'S MY NUMBER
SO CALL ME MAYBE

Pontiac, Illinois, like Joliet, was another one of those towns that owned its Route 66 heritage. Even the town's welcome sign was a large ROUTE 66 shield with the town's name stretched across the bottom. My guidebook said that there was a large Route 66 museum in the center of town.

It also recommended the "world famous" Three Roses Bed-and-Breakfast on Howard Street. I called to see if they had availability, which they did, so I walked the six blocks to the bed-and-breakfast.

The Three Roses was a beautiful, Victorian-style mansion with soft-gray, fish-scale shingles and white trimming. I knocked on the door, then walked inside, where I was greeted by Sharon Hansen, half the proprietorship of the Three Roses, which was named for the couple's three daughters.

Sharon led me to a room on the second floor. The view from the window was of the Vermilion River, spanned by one of Pontiac's three swinging bridges — an ironwork suspension bridge with a wooden walkway. She left me in my room, and I put away my things and laid back on the bed to rest a bit before dinner. I slept until the next morning.

CHAPTER THIRTEEN

I'VE COME TO UNDERSTAND THAT ROUTE 66 IS NOT A LOCATION — IT'S AN IDEA. IT'S THE PHYSICAL MANIFESTATION OF THE AMERICAN DREAM.
— CHARLES JAMES'S DIARY

I woke the next morning to the aroma of breakfast pleasantly wafting up to my room. I'm sure this was by design, as one of the B&B's slogans is "Where breakfast is an event!" (Exclamation added by proprietor.)

I went downstairs. The menu included egg and cheese strata, cinnamon rolls, seven kinds of pancakes — including oatmeal, flaxseed, butter pecan, and orange — French toast, Belgian waffles, fresh fruit, spiced oatmeal, homemade granola, and grits.

I ate a hearty breakfast, thanked Sharon for her hospitality and designer pancakes, grabbed my pack, and continued on my walk, stopping just a few blocks from the B&B at Pontiac's Route 66 Museum.

The museum, also called the Route 66 Hall of Fame, was well laid out. Its main floor displayed life in the 1930s and '40s with rooms representing the décor of the time — like a traditional dining room with rose-colored upholstered couches, a black lacquered bookshelf, and a console radio with rabbit-ear antennae.

There was also a kitchen, complete with a vintage refrigerator and stove, other appliances, and boxes and tin cans of the foodstuffs of that time.

As I looked over the displays, it occurred to me that Route 66 was a destination less of locale than of time — a 2,500-mile display case of an era.

In front of the museum was the Bob Waldmire Road Yacht, a school bus turned motor home with a wood siding exterior. Bob Waldmire was a Route 66 enthusiast who gained notoriety for touring up and down the Route in a mustard-colored VW microbus called the Old Route 66 Mobile Information Center.

I spent about an hour at the museum, though I could have stayed longer had I not been concerned with reaching my next destination. I left the museum and continued down Howard, turning left onto Route 23/Route 66.

It was along this stretch that I finally settled on the fact that there is not just one Route 66. Route 66, like the country it was built on, has never stopped evolving. When it first opened in 1927, parts of the original road, like all highways of the time, were gravel or graded dirt. The US Highway 66 Association (this may be the only road in history with a fan club) pushed to make it the first fully paved interstate in America. In 1930 much of the Route underwent major realignments, especially between Illinois and Missouri and particularly in St. Louis. Then, in 1932, it changed again.

Not surprisingly, the original road was smaller than the later versions, narrower and more precarious. One section was called Bloody 66 (owing to the frequency and lethality of accidents there), and a few places on the Route were so steep that the automotive technology of the day, with gravity-fed carburetors, required that cars drive backward to make it up the hills.

Since the older road was abandoned long before the rest of the highway, miles of road are still visible but unusable — the pavement broken up, with weeds and trees growing through the cracks.

My afternoon walking was easy, as the terrain was flat and the temperature pleasant. About nineteen miles into the day, the original two-lane road suddenly appeared again. Oddly, only one half of the road had been repaved.

I spent the night at the humbly named America's Best Value Inn, which boasted that it was the number one ranked hotel in Chenoa. It was also the only hotel in Chenoa.

CHAPTER FOURTEEN

**ART IS AN EXPRESSION OF LIFE.
PERHAPS IT SHOULD BE
THE OPPOSITE.
— CHARLES JAMES'S DIARY**

It was hard to believe that it had only been a week since I had left Chicago. It felt longer, much longer. As they say, it's not the years, it's the mileage.

I looked different. I had already lost weight, my beard was filling in, and my skin was toned a deep bronze. More importantly, I felt different. Curiously, being transient made me feel more stable. The next morning I passed more Burma-Shave signs.

WHEN YOU CAN'T SEE
PASSING CARS
MAY GIVE YOU A GLIMPSE
OF ETERNITY
BURMA-SHAVE

107

DON'T STICK YOUR ELBOW
OUT TOO FAR
IT MIGHT GO HOME
IN ANOTHER CAR
BURMA-SHAVE

Even though it was nearly summer, a decorated Christmas tree stood next to a billboard that read

GET YOUR KICKS ON TOWANDA'S
ROUTE 66

Two hours from Chenoa I reached Towanda. I couldn't see the name without envisioning Kathy Bates in the *Fried Green Tomatoes* movie shouting "Towanda!" before ramming her car into the car of the teenager who had just stolen her parking space.

THE WOLF IS SHAVED
SO NEAT AND TRIM
RED RIDING HOOD
IS CHASING HIM
BURMA-SHAVE

I didn't stop in Towanda, but continued on for four more hours until I reached the Bloomington-Normal water tower.

Bloomington and Normal are different towns, but up to that point, all the road signs I'd encountered had hyphenated them together like conjoined twins. Maybe they were. I wasn't sure where one town started and the other ended, but I learned that no one else did either.

The natives call the region Blo-No, which is a considerable savings of syllables but sounds like it needs a Kleenex.

Bloomington has a colorful past. It is the birthplace of both the Republican party and Beer Nuts — read into that what you will. The fictional character Colonel Henry Blake from the TV show *M*A*S*H* was from Blo-No, as was the American writer and philosopher Elbert Hubbard. While Hubbard may not be a common name among most Americans, he was a wise and unlikely hero of mine.

Hubbard was a fascinating character who described himself as both an anarchist and a socialist but was later disavowed by the Socialist Party when he became a vocal proponent of free enterprise and the American dream. When his anticapitalist friends accused him of selling out, Hubbard replied that he had not given up his ideals, he had "just lost faith in Socialism as a means of realizing them."

In addition to his more incendiary thoughts, he said many things that I found memorable and profound, some of which have stuck in the American lexicon. You have likely heard some of them and not known who they came from.

God will not look you over for medals, diplomas, or degrees — but for scars.

Don't take life too seriously. You'll never get out of it alive.

And a quote oftentimes misattributed to Aristotle:

Do nothing, say nothing, and be nothing, and you'll never be criticized.

What intrigued me most about Hubbard's life was how, in the end, his reality imitated his art.

After the sinking of the *Titanic,* Hubbard recorded the story of one Ida Straus, a married woman who, when offered a place on a lifeboat before the men, refused to leave her husband, choosing instead to die with him. Of the incident Hubbard wrote, "There are just two respectable ways to die. One is of old age, the other is by accident. Disease is indecent, suicide is atrocious. But to die as

110

Mrs. Straus did is glorious. Few have such a privilege, happy lovers both." The article ended with his now-immortal words, "In life they were not separated and in death they are not divided."

As he wrote those words, he couldn't have known that he was foreshadowing the circumstances of his own death. Three years after the *Titanic*'s sinking, the Hubbards boarded the ill-fated *Lusitania* in New York City. Eleven miles off the coast of Ireland the ship was torpedoed by a German U-boat.

Ernest Cowper, one of the survivors of the tragedy, offered this firsthand account:

After the ship had been torpedoed, Mr. and Mrs. Hubbard came up to the portside boat-deck. Neither appeared disturbed in the least. The Hubbards linked arms and stood looking calmly out over the side. Mr. Hubbard said to me, "Well, they have got us. They are a damn sight worse than I ever thought they were." When I asked what they were going to do, Mrs. Hubbard smiled and replied, "There does not seem to be anything to do." Then the two of them, still arm and arm, went into one of the rooms on the top deck and shut the

111

door behind them. It was the last they were ever seen.

They walked their talk and died *gloriously* together. As sad as their story was, to me it was also remarkably beautiful. The idea of loving someone, and being loved by someone, until death and beyond seemed almost unfathomable to me. It was something I wanted but told myself didn't really exist. I suspect that I was trying to protect my heart from the truth that, in my current state, I would be dying alone.

Bloomington is, among other things, a college town, the home of Illinois State University. With a population of about seventy-eight thousand, it's Illinois's twelfth-largest city, but combined with Normal, it's the fifth-most populous.

I began to feel a little claustrophobic as my solitary walking gave way again to crowded streets, honking horns, and jostling traffic. I found the hubbub wearisome.

I stopped at a Kroger's for supplies — mostly protein bars and water — then made my way to the Burr House, a stately red-brick bed-and-breakfast with gables and green-shuttered windows with flower boxes, and retired for the evening.

Chapter Fifteen

**Something Has Changed.
It's as If the Road Has
Begun Traveling Me.
— Charles James's Diary**

It was day eight of my walk, and I felt trapped in the city. Even one that was only a fraction the size of Chicago. Coming from a small life, I prided myself in having become cosmopolitan. I boasted that I was at ease in London, Paris, Rome, Chicago, but I now wondered if that was really true. Part of me yearned for solitude.

An hour into my walk there appeared a frontage road with a narrow bikeway that was perfect for walking. A little after noon I passed a sign that read,

MAPLE SIRUP
1/4 MILE AHEAD
FUNKS GROVE COUNTRY STORE

113

It was one of many signs I'd passed advertising Funks Grove maple syrup, which made me want some even though I didn't know what I'd do with it. Maybe it was the technically correct but unusual way they spelled *sirup.*

A few minutes later I reached the Funks Grove store's driveway. There was a Route 66 roadside attraction sign as well as a large wooden one announcing the store.

I followed the driveway up only to find the parking lot deserted and the store closed. A sign near the store read,

Sorry, We Are Sold Out

I felt cheated. I walked another ninety minutes until I came to the town of McLean, which pretty much consisted of a Hunts Brothers Pizza and a Super 8 Motel, and called it a day.

CHAPTER SIXTEEN

IT'S MY BIRTHDAY. IT'S A GRIM REALITY TO KNOW THAT THERE ARE FEWER CELEBRATING MY BIRTHDAY THAN THERE ARE CELEBRATING MY DEATH.
— CHARLES JAMES'S DIARY

The first town I reached the next day was Atlanta. Not *the* Atlanta; this one had a population of fewer than two thousand. The most notable resident of the town was a twenty-five-foot-tall fiberglass Paul Bunyon holding a massive hot dog. This is the exact same giant "muffler man" figurine that can be found in other towns and with different accoutrements throughout America — like the rocket-holding Gemini Giant I'd walked past at the defunct Launching Pad burger stop in Wilmington.

My guidebook said that there are 180 of these statues still in existence. The original giant statues held an ax, but they can be found holding just about anything from giant hot dogs to mufflers. I could fully imagine some future civilization uncovering these hulking creatures and concluding that they were gods our people worshipped. This giant Paul Bunyon (purposely misspelled with an *o* instead of an *a* for trademark reasons) was brought to Atlanta, Illinois, after the closing of Bunyon's Hot Dog establishment in Cicero, a suburb of Chicago and home to mob boss Al Capone, who moved to Cicero to escape the reach of Chicago police. There is no evidence that this giant fiberglass statue was in trouble with the law.

I continued walking, and two and a half hours later I reached Lincoln, Illinois. Interestingly, the city was named for Abraham Lincoln even before he became president. Lincoln is not a large town but big enough to have a Mel-O-Cream secret formula doughnut shop, where I stopped and ate a plain glazed doughnut. A mile later I passed the Route 66 Chapel. A sign on the door read,

Knock and it shall be opened to you.

Unfortunately, the building was locked

116

with a padlock and when I knocked, no one opened, which pretty much summed up my belief in and experience with God.

One thing that Lincoln, the town, is famous for (aside from its namesake) is the Railsplitter Covered Wagon. The twenty-four-foot-tall covered wagon, driven by a twelve-foot fiberglass statue of Abraham Lincoln, is the largest in the world, as attested to by the Guinness World Records certificate proudly displayed next to the wagon.

The wagon is a latecomer to the Route 66 attractions. It was built in 2001 and displayed along 66 in the small Illinois village of Divernon until 2007, when a Lincoln man purchased the wagon and donated it to the local tourism bureau. Two years later it was moved to its current location in the parking lot of a Best Western Hotel, where it was voted the number-one roadside attraction in America by *Reader's Digest* magazine.

I walked into the Best Western and booked my room. The clerk spent more time than I liked looking at my driver's license and had trouble running my credit card, making me wonder if it had finally been flagged. But a few moments later he checked me in, apologizing for their system, which he complained was notoriously slow.

I ate a light dinner, then stayed up late watching a documentary about the making of *Citizen Kane* and the war that ensued between genius actor and director Orson Welles and billionaire newspaper magnate William Randolph Hearst, who was famous for his yellow journalism and the line, "You provide the pictures, I'll provide the war."

The fallout from the battle of egos caused irreparable damage to both men and all but left Welles a broken recluse. Sadly, to most generations, Welles's legacy became his stint as pitchman for Paul Masson wines, with the memorable line, "We will sell no wine before its time." Welles was said to be inebriated during the recording.

The documentary left me thinking about my own life and legacy. These two men were world changers, men at the top of their games, dealing with fame, fortune, power, and glory. And they, like so many others in their situations, self-destructed. A long walk could have done them some good.

The next morning I lay in bed for a half hour before getting up. It was my birthday, May eighteenth. I shared the date with Hollywood director Frank Capra and Pope John Paul II. May eighteenth was also the day that Napoleon Bonaparte was crowned emperor of France. I always took that as a good omen.

I remembered that Amanda had celebrated my birthday before I left Chicago. Had we not, I wouldn't have been late to the airport and would have made my flight, making it my death day. I needed to remember to thank her for that when I got back.

I left the hotel before eight, following my map west on Lincoln Parkway. The road looked like an interstate and I walked along it for nearly three miles before spotting the original 66 running perpendicular to the highway.

There wasn't much to see on my walk. I passed three towns, including one called Broadwell, where a large granite rock bearing a plaque announced THE PIG HIP RESTAURANT 1937–1991. The restaurant was now a museum. I continued on, wondering if anyone ever stopped at the place.

After more than five hours of walking in solitude I came to Williamsville, where the Route turned off into a suburban neighborhood past a deserted Route 66 attraction called the Old Station — a simple gas station decorated in Route 66 memorabilia.

It was late afternoon when I reached Sherman. I walked a few more miles into

119

town, then stopped at the Pioneer Motel. I had put in a long day of nearly twenty-five miles. It was the one time that I would have gladly splurged for a massage if I could have found someone other than a truck driver to give it. Surprisingly there was a decent Thai restaurant nearby, where I told my waitress that it was my birthday. She brought me a complimentary dish of coconut ice cream with a candle in it.

CHAPTER SEVENTEEN

A MAN ONCE SAID TO ABRAHAM
LINCOLN, "I'M SORRY, BUT I'M
GOING TO HAVE TO SHOOT YOU."
"WHY IS THAT?" LINCOLN ASKED.
THE MAN REPLIED, "BECAUSE I
MADE A PROMISE THAT IF I EVER
SAW A MAN UGLIER THAN MYSELF, I
WOULD HAVE PITY AND KILL HIM."
LINCOLN REPLIED, "SHOOT AWAY,
SIR. IF I'M UGLIER THAN YOU, I
DON'T WANT TO LIVE."
— CHARLES JAMES'S DIARY

The next morning I entered the teeming
city of Springfield, Illinois, the sixth-largest
city in Illinois and the largest in central Illinois. Again, I wasn't looking forward to
the crowds but I was ready for some creature comforts, and I had already decided to
take a break once I reached the town. I
walked just half a day, checked into the

121

Springfield Hilton, took a hot shower, and set about doing my laundry.

The hotel was only a few blocks from the Lincoln-Herndon Law Offices Historical Site, where Abraham Lincoln and his partner worked from 1843 to1852.

Across from the law office is the Old State Capitol, where Lincoln wrote and delivered his "house divided" speech. It is also where his *twelfth* and final funeral was held before he was buried. At that time, the city of Springfield had a population of twelve thousand, and more than a hundred thousand people attended his funeral. His *twelfth.* I lived in a city of nearly three million people, and only seven showed up to mine.

The Abraham Lincoln Presidential Library and Museum was also only a few blocks from my hotel, so I decided to play tourist. The museum is designed with a circular plaza with different wings depicting different times of Lincoln's life, from the early log cabin years to the White House and the Civil War, replete with actual Lincoln family artifacts.

One exhibit showed a display of Lincoln political cartoons. I was surprised at how callously he was mocked by the papers of his time.

I reflected on the *Citizen Kane* documentary I'd watched a few nights earlier. Like both Hearst and Welles, Lincoln too was a man driven by ambition. Yet in Lincoln's case, that was what allowed him to endure his painful string of failures and defeats. He learned to turn a deaf ear to mocking and focused, instead, on the matters at hand.

Lincoln's goal was not, like Hearst's, to build an empire or to further fill his over-stuffed pockets. Nor was it like Welles's, to further inflate his own ego. Lincoln's priority was to serve his fellow man. And in deflecting self-aggrandizement, he received far more acclamation than Hearst or Welles could have ever dreamt of — a national monument in Washington and his face carved into a mountain by a grateful nation. Not surprisingly, more books have been written about Lincoln than about anyone else in human history except Christ.

There was one more thing about Lincoln I found interesting. It was something I already knew, but seeing the pictures of his funeral made it more real. Lincoln had dreamed of his death just a few days before it happened. What I hadn't heard is that Lincoln's cabinet recalled that, on the morning of his assassination, Lincoln had told them that he'd dreamed of sailing across an unknown body of water at great speed. It reminded me of my recurring dream. And here I now was, walking the road.

It was refreshing not having to reach a destination. I took my time, "sauntering," as Thoreau called it, walking around the town with no purpose other than to nourish my mental state. I felt remarkably light.

I ate dinner at the "famous" Obed & Isaac's Microbrewery. At my waitress's recommendation, I ordered the local special, the horseshoe — an open-faced sandwich on thick-sliced toasted bread, with grilled sirloin and cheese sauce topped with french fries. It was pretty much a heart attack sandwich and I loved every bite. It's one of the benefits of walking as much as I was. You don't have to watch your calories — just the traffic.

CHAPTER EIGHTEEN

**WE ALL HAVE TWO STORIES —
THE JOURNAL OF OUR LIFE
EVENTS, AND THE FICTION WE
TELL OURSELVES ABOUT THEM.
— CHARLES JAMES'S DIARY**

As much as I enjoyed my brief respite, I was back to walking the next day. The next four days were uneventful, so there wasn't much to write about. I checked off a few Route 66 attractions: I ate catfish and coleslaw at the Ariston Café — the oldest café on Route 66 — and passed the Soulby Shell station. But my most memorable stop was in Staunton, Illinois. There was an old, defunct gas station and a sign along the side of the road that said,

HENRY'S RABBIT RANCH

The ranch had a large yard with various attractions, including a poor man's version of the Cadillac Ranch — six Volkswagen Rabbits buried hood-first into the ground.

Four signs hung above the station:

WASCALLY WABBITS
GET THEIR KICKS
MEETING FOLKS
ON 66

The station had four weathered gas pumps. The pumps were more recent than many I'd seen at the vintage gas stations I had passed on my way, but not too modern. The price of gas was $0.63, and the Total Sale numbers only had one space for dollars, meaning the most you could spend on gas was $9.99. I guess back then they couldn't comprehend a tank of gas costing more than that.

A sign on the building advertised souvenirs and cold sodas, which sounded like a good enough reason to go inside. A brass bell clanged as I entered and the spring-loaded door slammed shut behind me. The room was about as cluttered as the yard, with Route 66 paraphernalia, maps, and books filling every available space.

A man wearing a white-collared shirt with suspenders stood behind the counter. He was holding a large rabbit, softly petting its short, brindled fur. The wood counter was half covered with brown shag carpet, the rest with a yellowed road map of Route 66. On the wall behind him was a framed, handwritten sign that read,

Please
No Discussions on
Politics or Religion
on Route 66.
Rabbits, that's okay.

Ironically, there was a political bumper sticker stuck to the front of the counter: a picture of a black rabbit next to an American flag, with the words

VOTE FOR MONTANA FOR PRESIDENT

I was looking at the sticker when the man spoke. "First time here?"

I looked up. "Yes, it is. Nice rabbit you've got there."

"His name's Henry."

"Is the place named after him?"

"Nah. He's not that old. I've only had him a few months. He was one of them rescued animals. Animal control took him from a woman who was a pet hoarder."

"I've heard of hoarders, but not pet hoarders."

"Same thing, only they do it with animals instead of old cans and junk. Crazy biddy. They've raided her home and taken her pets three times in the past three years. When I got Henry, here, she had one hundred ninety rabbits. Most of them damn near starving. Officers said the place stunk to high heaven."

"He looks well fed now."

"Oh, he's well fed, all right. Fat and sassy. Thinks he owns the place." He held the rabbit up by its torso so its legs dangled. "Look at that figure." He looked back at me. "But you probably didn't stop just to yak. If you did, you come to the right place, but what can I get you? I got a whole table of Route 66 patches over there, look good on that pack of yours. You out walking the Route?"

I nodded. "Westbound. I started in Chicago."

He petted his rabbit. "Thought so. You look like a Route walker. Not a lot of you out there, but I see you from time to time. Tell you what, I got pins too, if that's your thing. A lot of people like to collect 'em. 'Specially the younger folk."

"Thanks, but I just want something cold to drink."

"Got some cold sodas in the fridge. Guess that's redundant. If they're in the fridge, they better be cold. Ever heard of Route Beer, the *route* spelled with a *u* like Route 66?"

I nodded. "I had some back in Joliet. Is that what you have?"

"No, don't sell it. I got some colas and ginger ale."

"I'll take a ginger ale," I said.

He walked over to a refrigerator, which was the kind you'd find in a house, not a public stop. It was white and covered with dirty handprints. He crouched down a little to look through it, then brought over a bottle of Fanta Orange soda. He set it down on the counter in front of me. "Here you go. Icy cold and satisfying."

"That's not ginger ale," I said.

"Yeah, I'm out of 'em."

"I guess I'm drinking orange soda."

"It's good, you'll like it. I had some Europeans in here a while back. Nothing unusual about that, I get more Europeans in here than I do Americans — Americans don't know what they got in their own backyard — but these Europeans told me they got orange Fanta in Europe, but it isn't the same as it is here. They say it's sweeter here.

"Never been to Europe, so I couldn't tell you that for sure, but wouldn't surprise me.

Americans are addicted to sugar. We eat more of it than anywhere else in the world. I read somewhere that the average American eats a hundred and seventy pounds of sugar a year. That's the same as the average weight of an American woman. Course it used to be a lot less."

"The weight of women or the sugar consumption?"

"Both," he said. "And you can be sure there's a connection there."

"I've been to Europe," I said. "But I couldn't tell you if the Fanta tastes different."

"I've got no reason not to trust the Europeans. 'Cept the French. Still, you'd think they'd keep the soda all the same."

I took a sip of the drink. "You would think so."

"Don't know if you read about it in the paper, but a few years back I ran one of my rabbits for president of the United States. I figured she had a shot. She was the perfect candidate. Black like Obama, female like Clinton, and old like McCain."

I smiled. "This is your campaign bumper sticker?"

"Yes, it is."

"How did the campaign go?"

"I don't need to tell you she lost. Two-party system, an independent rabbit doesn't have a chance."

I nodded. "I look forward to the day when a nonpartisan rabbit can sit in the Oval Office."

"You and me both," he said. "You and me both."

I grinned. "Politics aside, how's business?"

"Good. And heating up. Always heats up with the weather. One day last summer I had twenty-two cars stop in one day. I think that's some kind'a record." He set down the rabbit. It took two small hops to the edge of the counter and stopped. "Don't worry, he won't jump off. Rabbits don't like heights." He looked at me. "Fascinating creatures, rabbits. Do you know what a baby rabbit is called?"

"A bunny?"

"Kittens. The proper term is *kittens*. I'm a living encyclopedia on rabbits. I know all sorts of useful facts about 'em. Many not so useful as well. You probably didn't know that more than half the world's rabbits live in North America."

"You're right. I didn't know that."

"They're a big part of American history. Around the time of the Great Depression, jackrabbits darn near overran a few states. It was apocalyptic. They traveled in herds and reproduced every thirty-two days. They wiped out entire farms in a day.

"The farmers and ranchers who settled the land had chased off all the coyotes and wolves, so there was nothing to keep the rabbit population from growing. By some estimates, they figured there were ten million rabbits just in western Kansas."

"That's a lot of rabbits," I said.

"You said it. At first the government put bounties on the hares' heads, but it about bankrupted them. Then farmers took to selling rabbit pelts, but pretty soon they were more plentiful than bad drivers in Missouri and the pelts wasn't worth the cost of the bullet they shot it with.

"So the people started jackrabbit drives. Townspeople would gather in a big ol' circle and start yellin' and stompin' and close in the circle until they got a few thousand rabbits in one big pile and then they'd club 'em to death. One drive had more than ten thousand people making that circle. Killed every rabbit in an eight-mile square."

"Sounds brutal," I said.

"Yeah, everyone cries brutality until it's their problem. People outside the area called the farmers barbarians. But the farmers just said, 'Fine, we'll just send them your way.' Well, that shut 'em up real fast. People still that way, finding motes in people's eyes when they got a castle stuck in their own.

"Ya know somethin' else that's peculiar about rabbits? Their teeth never stop growing. If they didn't grind them all the time, they'd have tusks. I'm not making that up. Fact is, I had a rabbit with tusks. Called him Woolly, like a woolly mammoth, 'cause of the tusks.

"He wasn't even that old either — and rabbits live upwards of ten years. Wish I still had Woolly. People would pay handsomely to see a rabbit with tusks.

"Speakin' of tusks, ya know, some scientists are on the verge of bringin' back the woolly mammoth? They found some mammoths up in ol' Siberia, frozen in ice; that's where they got the DNA. They're gonna splice and dice it, then do what they do with a modern elephant and whammo, instant mammoth. Scares me some. You never know when they're gonna start makin' elephant people or ratmen or some such nonsense."

"They could make rabbit people," I said.

His brow furrowed. "Can't say it wouldn't be an improvement. But it ain't the way God intended. You know Hitler tried some of that monkey business during World War II. Experimenting with apes and humans, trying to make a better soldier, one who didn't complain and who he could feed bananas to . . ."

I decided his mind was as eclectic as his station. "So how did you come to like rabbits so much?"

"I don't know. How'd you come to liking walkin' so much?"

"That's a good question."

"I thought so. I can see why you'd choose to walk Route 66. Thing is, it's not just a road, it's a club. Longest club in the world, stretchin' two thousand miles and then some. You'll meet people all along the way who want to be friends. Some of 'em years later still send me Christmas cards."

"Really?"

He looked at me seriously. "Wouldn't joke about a thing like that."

If I had a Christmas card list, this man would definitely be on it, I thought. I finished my Orange Fanta, left him the bottle to collect the deposit, then returned to the Route.

CHAPTER NINETEEN

WE NEVER KNOW WHAT HORRIFIC
AND POWERFUL CURRENTS RUN
BENEATH THE SEEMINGLY CALM
SURFACE OF ANOTHER'S LIFE.
— CHARLES JAMES'S DIARY

Two days later I reached the border of Illinois and Missouri, the first of eight state lines I would be crossing before I reached my destination. St. Louis and its famous Arch were visible in the distance.

The freeway leading from Illinois to St. Louis was too dangerous (and illegal) to walk, so I stuck out my thumb. I got picked up by an older model Chevy truck with a Southern Cross decal in the back window. The driver was about my age and owned a small remodeling company. He offered to take me into the city but I demurred, telling him that I wanted to walk as much of the Route as I could.

He dropped me off in a rough-looking area near the Chain of Rocks bridge, which, according to my guidebook, was part of the original Route 66 and one of the largest pedestrian bridges in the world. Originally it had been built for cars but had been closed off to vehicular traffic for almost fifty years. The mile-long bridge spans the Mississippi River as well as the Illinois–Missouri border and features a thirty-degree turn midway through.

The air was hot and moist. It took me a little less than twenty minutes to cross the bridge, passing fewer than a dozen other people, most on bicycles, on my way.

The opposite end of the bridge looked even more blighted than the Illinois side where I'd entered, and the parking lot was littered with trash and marked with graffiti. I headed south on Riverside Road.

St. Louis was still far enough away that I would either have to find a place to stay or walk after dark, though neither possibility looked promising, as the area looked more like a postapocalyptic war zone than suburbia. Everywhere I looked the buildings were boarded up or windows were broken out, and it seemed that everything — from benches to light poles — was covered with layers of graffiti, as if the area had broken out in a rash of spray paint.

Suddenly, an older silver Dodge Stratus pulled up to the curb next to me. The car had a dented back end and was missing its hubcaps. The driver, a midtwenties black woman, shouted to me. "Excuse me, sir."

I walked up to the car. "Yes?"

"You shouldn't be walking here."

"In this neighborhood?"

"This whole area. It's not safe. Where are you going?"

"I'm going into the city. I'm staying at a hotel near the Arch."

"Well, you'd better get in. I'll give you a ride. You can put your backpack in the backseat."

"You don't have to do this," I said.

"I think I do."

"Thank you." I opened her car's back door. As I took off my pack, she said, "I'm not going to steal your pack."

I laid my pack across the seat, then got in front. "I didn't think you would," I said.

The car seats were vinyl and warm, the air conditioner impotently fighting the sweltering heat. The woman glanced in her rearview mirror, put her car in drive, waited for a car to pass, and pulled out into the street. She was quiet for a moment. Then, without looking at me, she asked in a soft voice,

137

"Did you come over the bridge?"

"Yes." I looked at her, really seeing her for the first time. She was a little hard-looking, but pretty. "Have you ever walked over it?"

"Yes," she said shortly, keeping her eyes fixed on the road. After another minute she breathed out slowly, almost like a sigh. "Where in the city are you going?"

"The Hyatt Regency by the Arch. It's on —"

"I know where the Arch is," she said.

She continued to drive. The farther south we went, the more evident it was that the woman knew the area and its potential danger.

"What's your name?" I asked.

"Monika. With a *k.*"

"Monika? Really?"

"Yes, sir. What's yours?"

"Charles. Without a *k.*"

"Do your friends ever call you Chuck?"

"Not if they want to still be my friends."

Her shoulders loosened slightly. "Nice to meet you, Charles."

"My pleasure, Monika." We drove a bit more in silence. Then I said, "My wife was named Monica."

"Was? She changed her name?"

"She changed her marital status. We're divorced."

"Sorry." She turned toward me. "Is that a bad thing?"

"It was for me. I miss her."

"I'm sorry," she said again. A moment later, she said, "That's a big pack. Is it heavy?"

"By the end of the day it is."

"Where are you walking from?"

"Chicago."

"You walked all the way from Chicago?"

"Yes, ma'am."

"How many miles is that?"

"A little over three hundred."

"That's a long way to walk. Where are you walking to?"

"Santa Monica, California."

She glanced at me skeptically, as if waiting for me to tell her I was just kidding. "You're walking all the way to California?"

"Yes, I am."

"How far is that?"

"About twenty-five hundred miles."

"That is crazy." She glanced quickly at me. "I'm not saying you're crazy."

"I probably am."

"What's in California?"

"My ex-wife."

"You're walking twenty-five hundred miles to see your ex-wife?"

"Yes."

"You really do miss her," she said softly. A moment later, she added, "That's romantic. I'd like it if a man walked twenty-five hundred miles to see me."

"I hope she thinks so."

A few minutes later the Gateway Arch came into view, its stainless steel exterior reflecting the late-afternoon sun in brilliant, blinding flashes.

"I'll never get tired of looking at that," I said.

"Have you ever been inside?"

"Once. A long time ago."

"That elevator they made for it is remarkable. There are some smart people in this world." She paused. "Were you planning on walking all the way to St. Louis tonight?"

"Yes."

"Two nights ago they found a body about a mile from where I picked you up." She paused. "You're from Chicago; you get crime up there."

"I usually stay out of places they find bodies," I said.

"That would be nice."

"What do you mean?"

"That's where I live."

The downtown traffic was heavy and it took almost fifteen minutes just to navigate a few miles of the rush-hour traffic leading to the hotel. She pulled into the hotel's curved driveway and put her car in park. "There you go."

"Thank you," I said. "How can I thank you?"

"You just did."

"Have you had dinner?"

"No. I was just going home to make something."

"Come have dinner with me. My treat. There's a Ruth's Chris inside."

She shook her head, drumming her fingernails on the steering wheel. "That's okay."

"Have you ever eaten at Ruth's Chris?"

"No. I've heard of it, but never been there."

"I didn't think so."

She narrowed her eyes. "Why, because I drive a POS car?"

"No, because if you had, you wouldn't have refused dinner there. Unless, of course, you just didn't want my company."

"If I didn't want your company, I wouldn't have picked you up."

"You didn't know me back then."

"I still don't know you."

"Another reason to have dinner with me. Come on. Come have dinner with me."

She thought for a moment, then said, "All right. Where do I park?"

"These guys will take care of it," I said, gesturing to a valet. I got out of the car and lifted my pack from the back seat. One of the valets approached me.

"Will you be checking in, sir?"

"Yes. Not her, just me. We're going to have dinner first, so you can check my pack."

"Of course, sir. And what is your name?"

"Charles James," I said.

"Charles James," he repeated. Then he added, "Like the seminar guy."

His comment stopped me. "Seminar guy?"

"Oh, it's just this guy who goes around doing wealth seminars. He was here about a month ago."

I was waiting for him to recognize me. He didn't. "And you went to his seminar?"

The valet put a tag on my pack. "Yes. The whole thing."

"How was it?"

"It was good. He was a cool guy. He's like the grandson of Jesse James the outlaw. I didn't buy anything yet; I'm still saving up for the packages. It's almost ten grand, so it's going to take everything I've saved for the last two years."

I handed him a five-dollar bill. "Let me give you another tip. Hang on to your money."

He took my backpack, and Monika and I

walked inside. Being inside the hotel lobby brought back memories. It was the same restaurant I'd been at with McKay when he told me he was dying. The hostess sat us at a booth near the back of the restaurant, leaving us with dinner menus and a wine list. I sensed that Monika didn't feel comfortable in the setting.

I lifted the wine list. "Would you like some wine?"

"No thank you," she said.

"You don't like it?"

"I'm more of a beer drinker."

"Then how about a beer?"

"I'm okay," she said.

A moment later a waitress walked up to our table. "How are you folks tonight?"

"Well," Monika said.

"We're good," I said. "How are you?"

"I'm fine, thank you. May I get you something to drink?"

"Just water, please," Monika said.

I set down the wine list. "I'll have a glass of the Faust cabernet sauvignon."

"A very good choice. Are you ready to order?"

I glanced at Monika and said, "Give us a few minutes."

"Very good. I'll get you your drinks." She walked away.

Monika looked at the menu, her brow furrowed.

"Are you okay?" I asked.

She breathed out slowly. Finally she said, "This is how much I spend on food in a week."

"Then it's a good thing you're not paying for this," I said.

"You sure you can afford this?"

"Oh yeah," I said. "Can't you tell I'm rich?" Considering that I looked homeless, the rhetorical question sounded more like a joke.

"I'll take your word for it." She continued studying the menu.

After a moment I asked, "Is this weird, having dinner with a stranger?"

"Yes."

"With a *white* stranger?"

She hesitated. "Yes."

"Technically, I'm half Mexican."

The waitress returned with my wine. She set the glass in front of me, then gave us both ice-filled glasses of water. "Are you ready to order?"

"I think so," I said. "Monika, you first."

She set down the menu. "I'll have the wedge salad."

"What dressing would you like with that?"

"Blue cheese."

"And what would you like for your main course?"

"I'll just have the salad," she said.

I took a sip of my wine and said, "You're having more than that."

"No, I'm fine."

"Are you vegetarian?"

"No."

I set down my glass. "I can see I'll have to order for her. I'll have the cowboy ribeye. Medium rare. With a side of your sweet potato casserole and calamari." I looked at Monika. "And she will have your filet mignon, with a side wedge salad, with blue cheese. How do you like your steak, Monika? Burnt or rare?"

"In between."

"Medium, and another glass of wine for the lady. This is good."

The waitress said, "Very good. Thank you." She gathered our menus and left.

I turned to Monika. "Sorry, I had to take the wheel. I wasn't going to eat all that food in front of you."

"It's okay. Thank you." She was quiet for a moment, then asked, "Are you expecting something out of this?"

"Something?"

She just looked at me.

I smiled. "I expect you will enjoy dinner

immensely."

She laughed nervously.

"I'm already in your debt," I said. "You might have saved my life."

"I wasn't trying to be rude. I'm just not that kind of a girl."

"What kind of girl are you?"

"I'm a Christian one."

I nodded. "I understand."

"Do you have religion?" she asked.

"Rank and file agnostic," I said. "I was raised Catholic. I went to church every Sunday with my family, then came home and got beaten up by my old man. He beat God right out of me."

Monika frowned. "I was raised Baptist, but I left the faith for a long time."

"Why did you leave?"

Pain flashed in her eyes. She looked down, as if avoiding the question. A young man interrupted the silence, setting bread at our table and refilling our water glasses. He was followed by our waitress, carrying Monika's glass of wine. Monika took a sip of wine and said, "You really are walking to California?"

I knew that she had purposely dodged my question, so I didn't pursue it. "Yes. I really am."

"That's amazing. It must be nice to just

146

walk away. Sometimes I wonder why I don't just get on the next bus out of here and start somewhere else. But I never do. I go to my job, then come home, chain my door, and hope my car is there in the morning."

"Why do you think you don't leave?"

She slowly shook her head. "I don't know. Maybe I will if I ever put enough money away to give myself a cushion. I guess we trust the devil we know more than the one we don't."

I took another drink of wine, then looked Monika in the eyes. "When I was seventeen, I got on the bus. Literally. I went to California with nothing but a few clothes and less than a hundred dollars to my name. I had no idea where I was going to go, other than away from my father. I met my ex-wife on the bus to California. Sometimes it seems like the universe provides for the bold."

"And sometimes not," she said.

Just then our waitress brought out our food. Monika cut a piece from her still-sizzling steak, speared it with her fork, and took a bite. "Oh, my."

Her reaction made me happy. "So it's good?"

"Heaven is good," she said. "This is amazing."

After we had eaten a while in silence,

Monika looked at me and said, "You asked why I left my faith . . ."

I stopped eating and looked up at her.

"My two little sisters were murdered on that bridge you walked over. They were only ten and thirteen. A group of boys raped and killed them, then dropped their bodies into the river."

The revelation sickened me. "I am so sorry."

She lifted her napkin from her lap and dabbed her eyes.

After a moment I asked, "How long ago was that?"

"About six years." She looked at me. "I miss them. Every day. They were such sweet girls. I couldn't believe that God would let that happen. I hated Him for that. I hated Him almost as much as I hated those boys."

"Did they catch the boys?"

"Yes. They're all in prison. The youngest was only sixteen, but they tried him as an adult."

"So why did you go back to church?"

"I needed it. I found myself changing into the very thing I hated. That's what hate does — it remakes us in its image."

I thought over her words. "So you just went back?"

She shook her head. "No. That took a

while. I started by praying. I asked God to help me let go."

"Did it help?"

She dabbed her eyes with the napkin again, then said, "A couple of days after my prayer, I had a dream. I was in a beautiful park. It was perfect, with the sun shining and millions of wildflowers and a clear brook. Then suddenly my sisters were there with me. They were wearing beautiful gowns of brilliant white that somehow reflected different colors like a rainbow whenever they moved. But even more brilliant than their gowns were their faces. They were just looking at me. They looked so happy. Then Monique, the youngest of my sisters, said to me, 'We are at peace, Moni. Are you?'

"That's when I woke. It was so real." She looked into my eyes. "Do you believe in dreams? Like they might be real?"

"Maybe. A dream put me on this walk."

"I don't know if that dream was real or not, but the peace it brought me was real." She looked into my eyes. "Hating those boys didn't do anything to the boys, just to me. So I pushed them and all my hate from my heart. Once I did that, God came back in." She looked into my eyes. "Maybe He will with you too."

I took a deep breath and forced a smile.

"Maybe," I said. "Maybe."

As we were finishing our dinner, our waitress came back to our table. "Would you like some dessert this evening?"

I looked at Monika. "Dessert?"

"No, thank you. I'm very full."

"Just the check, please."

She looked at Monika's half-eaten steak. "Would you like a box to take that with you?"

"Yes. It will be my lunch tomorrow. Thank you."

I paid the bill, and we got up to go. "Thank you for dinner," Monika said.

"Thank you for picking me up. A complete stranger."

"It was my pleasure."

A few moments later we left the restaurant. I walked her outside the hotel. I handed the valet a ten-dollar bill and the valet ticket. Then I said to Monika, "Hold on a minute. There's something I want to give you."

"I'll wait," she said.

I ran back into the hotel and retrieved my backpack from the bag check, took out some money, then went back outside. By the time I got back, Monika's car had come and she was standing on the opposite side

150

of the car looking for me.

"Sorry to keep you," I said. "I wanted to give you this." I handed her ten one-hundred-dollar bills.

She looked at the money, then back up at me. "What is this for?"

I smiled. "The bus."

Chapter Twenty

The Human Need to Attach Ourselves to Land Makes Me Wonder If We Ever Own Real Estate or It Really Just Owns Us.
— Charles James's Diary

The next morning I found myself thinking about my conversation with Monika. I wondered if she really would get on the bus. I hoped she would. Whether she did or not, I was sure she could use the money.

I ate a light breakfast in the hotel lobby, then started out, fighting my way out of downtown St. Louis through both human and automotive traffic. The farther I got from the city, the more pleasant the walking (and breathing) as asphalt and concrete gave way to grass and trees.

A little after noon, I left the freeway, following a sign to the Route 66 State Park.

The park's visitors center was located in an old roadhouse. It was run by a woman named Madeleine who introduced herself to me as "the ambassador of the 66." Even though I had little interest in the building she occupied, Madeleine had enough passion for both of us and told me about the place in excruciating detail.

Built in 1937, the two-story building had once been a bar and restaurant called the Bridgehead Inn. People came to the inn to escape the summer heat of St. Louis. And to gamble. Maybe just to gamble.

The park was built on land once called the Times Beach — a questionable vacation spot that the *St. Louis Times* newspaper gave away plots of. People's houses were built on stilts because the place frequently flooded.

As the area started to grow, people began to mysteriously get sick and it was discovered that dioxin, a highly toxic compound, had been used in the construction of the roads. This revelation was followed by a mass exodus of residents. In 1982, the final hammer fell when a flood decimated the town.

"The government stepped in and bought people out," Madeleine said. "They were more than fair." She looked me over. "You're following the Route?"

"Yes."

"East to west?"

"Yes."

"Good. It's the only way to do the Route. Be sure to stop at the Meramec Caverns. They're only an hour away from here." She looked me over again, then added, "At least, by car."

"It will take me a few days," I said.

"You know the caverns were the hideaway of the legendary outlaw Jesse James."

"I've heard that," I said.

"He used to go there during the Civil War when he was a bushwhacker. Then after the war he used the place as a hideout from the law. If you're interested, there's a Jesse James museum not far from it."

"I wouldn't go there," someone said. I looked over to see an old man standing near the front counter, leaning on his cane. "When I went there, there was a woman who just blabbered through the whole film. I couldn't hear a thing."

Madeleine frowned. "I don't think the woman will still be there, Vic."

"You never know. That biddy was like stink on manure."

"That was twenty years ago, Vic," Madeleine said. "Get over it."

"I'll check it out," I said.

I bought some cold bottled water and a bag of horehound candy, ate lunch at their café, and started back out on the road.

Near the end of my day the Route left 44, returning to the historic byway. I spent the night at a KOA in a kiddie train called the Kozy Kaboose. It didn't cost much.

The next two days were pleasant walking. I was glad to be off the highway and on wide, less-traveled roads where I wasn't constantly worried that I'd be killed by someone texting and driving.

The small towns I passed seemed to be clinging desperately to their pasts. Nearly every store or business had a Route 66 shield in its window or even took the name of the road, like Route 66 Taxidermist or Route 66 Realtors — "The shortest route to your new home."

But clinging to the past has never guaranteed tomorrow, and many of the towns I walked through looked to be in a terminal state, as if they couldn't make up their minds whether to live or die. I suppose, in a way, that described me as well.

Three days out of St. Louis, I reached the Meramec Caverns.

CHAPTER TWENTY-ONE

**IT'S CURIOUS TO ME HOW MANY WAYS PEOPLE HAVE PROSPERED OFF THIS HOLE IN THE EARTH.
— CHARLES JAMES'S DIARY**

The Meramec Caverns are roughly three miles off the Route, preceded by a long descent down a lush, oak-lined road with the Meramec River flowing to the north.

The caverns are a four-hundred-million-year-old limestone cavern system that stretches more than four and a half miles into the Ozarks. Today the caverns attract more than a hundred thousand visitors a year, making it the most visited of Missouri's many caves.

Initially the cave was valued as a source of potassium nitrate — commonly known as saltpeter — a chemical compound used in the creation of gunpowder. During the Civil War, the caverns were both mined for saltpeter and used as a factory by the Union army to secretly manufacture gunpowder, until the site was discovered by Confederate guerrillas, who ignited the stockpile of explosives, killing everyone inside.

My great-great-grandfather Jesse James was part of that Confederate attack. I assume it's how he became acquainted with the caverns as a hiding place.

I walked past several rental cabins into a twenty-acre parking lot with a zip line, gold-panning sluice, and fudge shop. The parking lot was crowded and a half-dozen school buses lined the east end. It was the largest group of people I'd seen since I left St. Louis, which made me feel a little claustrophobic. I ate lunch at the caverns' restaurant (which was decorated with pictures of Jesse and Frank James), then paid to go on a guided tour through the cave.

The cavern, once called Saltpeter Cave, was believed to be much smaller until the owner, Lester Dill, discovered a passage that led deeper into the mountain. He also discovered some old guns and a railroad strong box that was known to have been stolen by Jesse James and his gang. The box was now on display behind glass near the front of the cave.

Mr. Dill and I had much in common. In

fact, when it came to marketing, I would admit that he had me beat. He was a consummate promoter with a natural flair for publicity. He even invented the bumper sticker, first as a sign advertising his caves that schoolchildren tied with twine to the bumpers of cars, and then, after the invention of adhesive paper, actual decals.

He also drove Route 66 seeking out barns near the road and paying the farmers in whiskey, watches, and cave passes to let him paint the roofs or sides of their barns with the words MERAMEC CAVERNS ROUTE 66.

Once, in a gutsy display of promotional prowess, Dill climbed to the top of the Empire State Building and threatened to jump off if everyone in America didn't visit Meramec Caverns. After a few days he gave himself up to the police who were trying to talk him down.

He spent nine days in jail for the publicity stunt but garnered media attention for his attraction in hundreds of newspapers across America.

Dill and I had something else in common. We had both profited off my ancestor. After all these years, Jesse James was still getting people to hand over their money.

I spent the night in the Meramec Caverns

Motel. The next morning I left the grounds, stopping near the highway at the Jesse James Museum. A sign near the door asked, "Was Jesse James America's Robin Hood or a cold-blooded killer?"

Actually, James was a brutal killer with a good publicist. Himself. After one of his gang's bank robberies, he and his brother made a daring escape, which was publicized in newspapers across America, making them famous.

James leveraged his newfound celebrity by sending letters exclusively to John Newman Edwards, the editor and founder of the *Kansas City Times*.

In addition to the sensationalism of exclusive correspondence with a well-known outlaw and the newspapers that sold, Edwards had other motivations for printing the letters. He was a former Confederate soldier and was seeking to return former secessionists to power in Missouri. Edwards published dozens of Jesse's letters, asserting his innocence — letters which, through time, became more and more political.

In publicity, James was ahead of his time, spinning his image from cold-blooded murderer and bank robber into a Robin Hood–like folk hero. I wondered if that's where my marketing savvy had come from.

Inside the museum, I watched a movie that claimed that the real Jesse James hadn't died, as believed, in 1882 at the hands of Robert Ford. The movie asserted that Ford had killed another man and quickly buried him so that James could live in peace without the fear of a price on his head.

Not surprisingly, it was an assertion that the Meramec could profit from. By that time, Rudy Turilli, Dill's son-in-law, had taken over the caverns and, like his father-in-law, was always looking for the next big promotion. That's when he came across a man claiming to be Jesse James. Whether Rudy believed the man really was James or not, he found him convincing enough that he announced to the world that James was still alive. He threw a well-publicized party in the cave for the supposed James on his 102nd birthday.

Thousands of people turned out for the celebration. Many testified that the man was, indeed, Jesse James, including John Trammel, a 110-year-old black man who had worked as a cook for the gang.

The museum had some of my ancestor's artifacts, including an old bulletproof vest and — if it was him — the pearl-handled revolver given to him by Turilli at that birthday party.

I don't know what it is in the human psyche that celebrates criminals, but we are perverse in that way. I couldn't help but contrast the small plaque remembering the Reverend Christian Christiansen I'd come across in Gardner — a humble man who may have quietly helped to save the world — to the legacy of my great-great-grandfather. Today there are six museums and five festivals dedicated to Jesse James.

Over the next ten days I walked past nothing of exceptional interest. I wrote down a single list of unusual observations.

- Town of Bourbon. Home of the Bourbon virus, cause of a sometimes fatal disease. (Not sure I would have added that fact to a welcome sign.)
- The "world's largest rocker" in Cuba, Missouri.
- The Vacuum Museum. (Really. It was closed.)
- A miniature Stonehenge.
- The Uranus Fudge Factory. (No comment.)

In the town of Devil's Elbow, I stopped to eat at the Elbow Inn and Bar, a tiny pub hidden among trees at the edge of a forest.

I remember thinking, *This is the kind of place where you could disappear and never be found.*

When I walked in, the only other patrons were two women who were sitting at the bar drinking beer. Jimi Hendrix played on the jukebox.

I ordered the ribs, and the waitress brought out the largest rack of pork ribs I'd ever seen. While I was eating, a massive man walked into the bar wearing a hockey mask. I was pretty sure he was going to rob the place until one of the women said, "Whatcha doin' wearin' that getup?"

The man pulled off the mask, exposing a chubby, boyish face. "It's for fun. You should have seen those Swedish people that were in here earlier. They ran out without paying their bill." His smile turned to a frown. "Now Jed says I have to pay their bill or I can't drink here no more."

As he walked by me, I asked him his name. He looked at me defensively.

"Billy-Bob. What's it to you?"

"Have some ribs, Billy-Bob."

He looked at the ribs on my platter and said, "What's wrong with 'em?"

"There's nothing wrong with them. There are just too many."

"Why don't you just take 'em with you?"

"I'm walking," I said.

"Fair 'nuff." He sat down across from me and pretty much ate everything except the bones.

CHAPTER TWENTY-TWO

**SOME ATTACH THEMSELVES TO THE
ROAD TO MAKE THEMSELVES
LEGEND. OTHERS, ROADKILL.
— CHARLES JAMES'S DIARY**

Another uniquely Route 66 encounter was at the Munger Moss Motel in Lebanon, Missouri — a Route 66 icon. The hotel's welcome sign — with a brightly lit arrow that still advertised FREE TV — is a classic of the era's design and featured on many of the Route 66 posters and guidebooks I'd seen on my way.

The proprietors, Ramona and Bob, have owned the Munger Moss Motel for more than forty years. Ramona is another self-proclaimed keeper of Route 66 and an outspoken advocate, which I learned the moment I asked for a room.

"Where are you from?" she asked.

"Chicago."

"You doing the road?"

"Yes, ma'am."

"The road's a big deal. Did you know that there are museums in other countries for Route 66?"

"I didn't know that."

"It's true. People along the Route are practically legends. Once a Brazilian woman walked in here, took one look at me, and said, 'By damn, you're real.' " She glanced down at my pack. "You're not walking the Route, are you?"

"I have so far."

She shook her head. "Route walkers are crazy. Maybe when the road started it was okay, but in this day and age, you could just disappear. Nobody would ever find you. People are crazier than back then. I mean, they've always been crazy, but now you kind of expect it."

"I'm careful," I said.

She shook her head. "Even without the crazies, I'd never walk it. It's bad karma. If you push the road too hard, it's going to push back. People burn themselves out on 66. I've seen it. I knew a guy who did the Bunion Run back in the sixties — that's when they run the whole Route. Burned himself out. Almost had a breakdown. When he was through, he just disappeared. No one ever saw him again. He probably ended up in an institution somewhere weaving baskets, know what I mean?"

I guessed the question was rhetorical, as she didn't stop talking.

"I used to know people who'd do the Route five times a year, drive up and down, up and down. Now they do nothing."

I was about to suggest that driving up and down the Route was pretty much the same as doing nothing, but again she didn't pause long enough for me to speak.

"To me, going down Route 66 is to be savored, like sipping a fine wine. It's a pleasure cruise. It's meant to be peaceful. When you're on the Internet or in the world, it's all rush, rush, rush. Got to have more bandwidth, faster service, but Route 66, it's a Zen thing. It's peace. If you're in a hurry to drive it, you've already missed it. You've got to stop to talk to the people. Learn something about them. Why is everyone on Route 66 happy? I'll tell you why, it's because they're talking to each other. It's about the people."

I waited a moment to be sure that she had actually stopped talking, then asked, "How did you end up here?"

"Oh, the road and I were predestined, like star-crossed lovers. My husband's an auto mechanic. One winter he got caught in a blizzard at the shop with six other men. The power went out and they burned old rags in a barrel to keep warm. They had to break into the candy machine with lug wrenches to get something to eat. For two days they lived on Pop-Tarts and Red Vines. When he finally got out he said, 'Ramona, that's it. We're moving.'

"I said, 'Where, Bob?' He said, 'I don't know, Ramona. Somewhere else.' So we just picked up and left. On our way to somewhere else, fate had it that we stopped here at the motel and met the owners, Pete and Jessi. Well, Pete and Bob were both Masons, you know how that is. Next thing we know, we're making an offer and a month later we owned the place. Pete and Jessi stayed on awhile to teach us the ropes and the rest is history."

She took my cash and handed me a room key. "Route 66 won't ever die," she said, touching her heart. "Because it's not out there. It's in here."

I spent the night in a room with pictures of Route 66 sites adorning the redbrick walls.

As I walked out of my room the next morning, I saw a group of four men gathered around three vintage Corvettes.

"Where are you from?" I asked the man nearest me. He was leaning against an immaculately restored red Corvette convertible.

"Toronto."

"Beautiful car," I said. "Sixty-two?"

"Sixty-three."

I gazed at it admiringly. "I bet that cost a few loonies." I'd learned that slang for money during my Toronto seminars.

He smiled at my use of the word. "You're looking at my retirement," he said.

"You came all the way down from Canada to drive the Route?" I asked.

"We sure did."

"Why?"

A broad smile crossed his face. "Because it's there."

Like the long, lonely stretch from the Meramec Caverns to Lebanon, the 124 miles to my next destination — Joplin, Missouri — didn't have much to offer other than a whole lot of fresh air and old road.

That and a few oddities. I passed three unusual sites that I made note of in my diary.

The first was an old casket shop just outside Lebanon that was missing its roof. I don't know how long the stone block building had been abandoned, but the entire inside of it had grown into a forest.

Second was a dead possum that someone had put on top of a mailbox. It was fresh enough that it was covered with flies. When I told a shopkeeper in town about it he said, "Welcome to the Ozarks."

Third, I spent a night in the Boots Court Motel, a famous Route 66 attraction and the kind of place that still promoted itself with "a radio in every room." Apparently, Clark Gable had spent a night at the hotel, camping out in room 6. I asked to stay in room 6 but, not surprisingly, it was already occupied.

Three days from Lebanon, I walked into the populous city of Joplin and an encounter that changed my life.

CHAPTER TWENTY-THREE

I'VE MET A MAN WHO CLAIMS TO HAVE TALKED WITH GOD.
— CHARLES JAMES'S DIARY

The city of Joplin was named after a minister, but had he known what the town would become at the height of its mining boom, he probably would have asked for his name back. Shortly before the Civil War, lead was discovered in Joplin and mining camps began popping up around the city. This was followed a few years later by the discovery of a more valuable mineral, what the miners back then called "jack" — today known as zinc. Miners poured into the town and soon bars and brothels outnumbered the churches by ten to one. By the beginning of the twentieth century, Joplin had become a regional metropolis, as well as the lead- and zinc-mining capital of the world.

Today the city's mining past is still revealed by a landscape that had been remade with tailings piles and abandoned open-pit mines.

Joplin was also a favorite hangout of Bonnie and Clyde. Once, after the Joplin police had been tipped off to their whereabouts, the couple got away, killing two police officers in their escape. In their haste, they left a camera behind. The local newspaper developed the film in the camera, which led to the iconic pictures we have today of the two outlaws smiling and posing with machine guns.

I stopped at a pub near the center of Joplin, a few blocks from the hospital. There was an older gentleman, probably in his late sixties, sitting at the bar with a tall mug of dark ale. I sat down next to him. The long days alone must have been getting to me, because I was eager for conversation.

"What are you drinking?" I asked.

He nudged his glass. "Their Oatmeal Stout."

"How is it?"

"It's good," he said, then he took a drink as if he'd just remembered it was good. "Nothing better at the end of a stressful day."

"I hear you."

The bartender set a small plastic dish of

mixed nuts in front of me, and I ordered the same beer as the man was drinking.

After I ordered, the man turned to me. "Benjamin Franklin said, 'Beer is proof that God loves us.' "

"Beer *is* God," I said.

He looked at me as though my comment bothered him. "No, it's not," he said. "God is God."

"You're a believer in God?" I asked. "The big Santa in the sky?"

His brow furrowed. "The Santa in the sky?"

"Isn't that what God is? Just an adult version of Santa Claus. Didn't Freud prove that?"

"Freud proved what?"

The bartender set my beer down in front of me, and I took a drink. "That is good," I said.

"You were saying that Freud proved there is no God," the man said.

"Right. He said that God is just the manifestation of our deepest wishes. Especially the wish for security in a dangerous world. That's why we usually think of God as a man, since men are traditionally the protectors. Freud proved there is no God."

The man's brow again furrowed. "I don't think Freud's argument was that God didn't exist; it was more that our belief in Him is driven by our desire for Him to exist. Which, in fact, He does."

"You say that like you've seen God," I said, lifting my mug.

He looked at me for a moment, then said, "As a matter of fact, I have."

I set down my glass and looked at him, waiting for the punch line. None came. "You've seen God," I said.

He looked at me calmly. "Yes."

"What if I told you I thought you were crazy?"

He smiled. "Well, I did just come from the hospital's psych ward." He reached into his pocket and pulled out a business card.

Raymond George, MD
Chairman
Department of Psychiatry

I looked up from the card, feeling a little stupid that I'd been tossing around Freud with a professional. "You're a psychiatrist?"

"I'm the chairman of the department."

"Do they know you claim to have seen God?"

"Does *who* know?"

"Whomever you report to."

He nodded. "Yes. The hospital board and CEO all know."

"And they still gave you that job . . ."

He smiled. "I know. I'm still a little surprised that happened."

I took another drink, then turned back to him. "So tell me about God," I said flippantly. "What's he like? Does he wear tweed or is it all white robes and burning bush stuff? And if he didn't want Adam and Eve to eat the apple, why did he even make the tree?" I lifted my beer. "Tell me about him."

He looked at me for a moment and said, "No. I don't think I will." He turned back to his glass.

I looked at him incredulously. "Hey, you can't make a statement like that and not deliver."

He looked at me sternly. "You've already decided I'm either a fool or a liar, so why would I waste my time?"

It was difficult talking to someone whose life had been devoted to surfing people's minds. "What if I told you that I'll give you the benefit of the doubt?"

"Then I'd say *you* were a fool or a liar. Based on your reaction, I would seriously doubt you're capable of making such an abrupt paradigm shift."

"Fair enough," I said. "But all the same, I'm interested in what you think you saw."

His mouth rose in an amused smile. "What I *think* I saw?" He took another long draw from his mug, wiped his mouth with a napkin, then turned back and looked at me. His piercing blue eyes were nearly eclipsed beneath heavy gray caterpillar eyebrows. "All right. I'll share my experience. For your benefit, not mine. Do with it as you will."

"Thank you," I said.

"It was 1972, just a few weeks before the Vietnam peace agreement was signed in Paris. I was a newly recruited private in the air force. I was stationed in Biloxi, awaiting my assignment. It was just a little before Christmas, and I had been given a furlough to go home to Denver.

"Two days before my vacation, I came down with a fever and cough. It got worse fast. By the next day I was hospitalized with pneumonia.

"Suddenly I found myself feeling better and sitting by the side of my bed with a nurse running out of my room. I called out to her, but she ignored me. I followed her out to the corridor and shouted for her again, but again she didn't respond.

"There was another nurse walking toward me. I turned to her and said, 'I'm sorry, but

175

could you help me find my doctor? I'm supposed to be going home.'

"She didn't even look at me. It made me angry. I reached out to grab her arm, and my hand went right through her.

"At that point I had pretty much figured out that something was wrong. Then my nurse came running back with a doctor. I tried to get their attention, but they ran past me to my bed. That's when I saw that there was still someone in the bed. Someone who looked an awful lot like me.

"The doctor looked at my heart monitor, which looked crazy — like a bunch of radio waves — then grabbed the paddles and shocked my body. I watched my body nearly jump off the bed. He tried twice more; then the monitor started buzzing. The nurse said, 'He's asystolic.'

"I looked at the monitor. I had flatlined. The doctor started performing chest compressions. Then he and the nurse traded off. Finally, after five or so minutes, the doctor stopped. He was panting with exhaustion. He said, 'I'm calling it. He's gone.' I just stood there looking at them. 'I'm not gone,' I said. 'I'm right here. Keep doing it.'

"Then the nurse pulled the sheet up over my head. I shouted at them. 'Don't stop! I'm going home for Christmas. My parents are expecting me!' Almost as soon as I said that, I was above the hospital, moving at a tremendous speed. Even though I was flying over snow-covered mountains, I wasn't cold. In fact, I couldn't feel anything except motion.

"In less than a minute, I was standing in my parents' kitchen. My parents were sitting at the kitchen table. They had just finished dinner and my mother was asking my father what she should make for my homecoming dinner.

"He said, 'You know how he loves your stuffed peppers and rice.' Then he came over to help her with the dishes, and my mother said that she was going to tell me that Margaret Wright, a girl I had dated for a while, was marrying the Wallis boy, and hoped that I would take it all right. My mother then added, 'I never wanted them to marry anyway. Her mother is a closet lush.' My dad said, 'At least Margaret won't have to change her initials.'

"I'm telling you all this because I verified the entire conversation with them after I got home." He shifted a little in his chair. "The whole time I was trying to talk to them but they couldn't see or hear me. After a while I started thinking of my body, and suddenly I was transported back to the hospital in the same way I came. Considering that my parents lived almost fourteen hundred miles away in Denver and I'd traveled the distance in less than a minute, I was moving impossibly fast. I've done the math. I had to be moving faster than mach one hundred."

"Nobody could survive that much acceleration," I said.

"Then it's a good thing I was already dead," he replied, grinning.

I thought over his story, then said, "So where was your God in all this?"

He nodded. "That's exactly what I was wondering. I was suddenly back at the hospital standing next to my body, trying to figure out what to do next. I'm wondering, *Could this really be death, to just hang around the world with no substance?*

"Just then the room began to glow impossibly bright. Brighter than anything I'd ever seen or could have seen with my eyes without losing them.

"At first I wondered where the light was coming from, but then I realized it wasn't *where* but *who*. The light was coming from a personage standing in front of me. Then a voice said to me, *You are in the presence of the Son of God.*"

"Jesus," I said. "You saw Jesus Christ."

178

"Yes."

If he was lying, I couldn't see it. He told the story as calmly as if he were reciting what he'd had for dinner last night. True or not, I was convinced that he, at least, believed his story.

"Then what?" I asked.

"He asked me what I had done with my life."

"What did you say?"

"I said that I was just starting my life. I wasn't supposed to die this young. He said to me, 'Death can come at any time.' "

"Then what?"

"We left the hospital. He showed me things."

"What things?"

"Things I can't tell you."

"Really?" I said. "Like, you know the future?"

He smiled. "I didn't think you believed me."

"I didn't," I said. "But you're pretty convincing. So how did you come back to life?"

"That's a story in itself," he said. "In all I was gone just nine minutes. But it would have taken several days to see all that I saw."

"Nine minutes; you should be brain-dead."

"I've been accused of that as well," he said, slightly grinning.

"You have witnesses?"

"Many. And I have a signed death certificate. It hangs on the wall next to my doctorate degree. Everyone should have one. It's a good way to keep your priorities straight."

Meeting him felt like more than a coincidence. Both of us had been pronounced dead.

He finished his beer. After a moment he said, "You don't have to believe me. You don't have to believe anything. It doesn't change the truth of my experience.

"But if I can give you some advice, for your own sake, keep an open mind. There's a difference between not believing in the existence of a higher power and denying the existence of a higher power because you've blamed it for something that's happened to you."

I just looked at him with astonishment. "How did you know that something happened to me?"

"I didn't. But most of the people I meet who claim there is no God are really just angry at God and feel like denial is a way to get back at Him."

I took a much-needed drink. For a few minutes neither of us spoke. Then I turned to him. "I lost God after my father nearly beat me to death. I reasoned, if God wasn't powerful enough to stop him, He isn't a God. And if He were powerful enough to stop him, but doesn't, then He's not good."

The man nodded slowly and said, "That's an understandable rationale, but flawed."

"How so?"

"The greatest gift God could give us is free agency. Without it, there's no point of existence. We'd just be meat puppets. Would you agree with that?"

I thought about it, then nodded. "I can accept that."

"But you can't have it both ways. You can't allow free agency only if it agrees with your will. That's not free agency, it's control. So what is it, freedom or control?"

"You should have been a minister," I said.

"No, I don't like working Sundays. But I'd have to say that spending a few minutes on the other side trumps a lifetime in theological studies."

"And your bosses at the hospital really know about this?"

He smiled. "You would have enjoyed my job interview. I was interviewed by the hospital's CEO, a declared atheist. I was thinking that the interview was going well, when he crossed his arms, looked me in the eyes, and said, 'You're on record saying that you have seen God. Is that true?'

"I thought, *There it goes.* But I wasn't going to lie about the most significant event of my life. I certainly wasn't going to deny Him. So I looked the doctor in the eyes and said, 'Yes, it is true.'

"He looked at me for a moment, nodded, and said, 'All right, we'll get back to you.' Two days later they offered me the job."

"That's pretty remarkable," I said.

"That was more than eight years ago. Since then Dr. Probst, the CEO, and I have become close friends. About a year ago I reminded him about the interview. He laughed and said, 'Look, I didn't know if you'd seen God or what, but I did know that you were on record saying that you had. So if you'd denied it, you were not someone I could trust.' "

I thought for a moment. "So you're saying that God lets bad things happen because He loves us."

"Yes. It's a paradox."

"It's a terrible paradox," I said.

"It is, except when you consider the conclusion."

"What's that?"

"It's all temporary. In the end, love wins."

■ ■ ■ ■

I woke the next morning unable to get the conversation I'd had with the doctor out of my mind. Had he really had that experience? I believe that he believed it, but that doesn't make it true. I had heard about near-death experiences before, even once from a client, but I had always dismissed them as delusions of weaker minds. But this man's mind wasn't weak. And as far as I could figure out, he had no motivation to lie. I suppose that's what bothered me most of all. I couldn't figure out the man's angle.

CHAPTER TWENTY-FOUR

KANSAS CLAIMS A MERE
ELEVEN MILES OF ROUTE 66.
IT TOOK ME LESS THAN THREE
HOURS BEFORE I COULD SAY,
"TOTO, I'VE A FEELING WE'RE NOT
IN KANSAS ANYMORE . . ."
— CHARLES JAMES'S DIARY

Two and a half weeks from the time I crossed over the Mississippi River into Missouri, I walked out of the western side of the state, over the Kansas border.

Of the eight Route 66 states, Kansas has the least amount of road, with just eleven miles of asphalt crossing through the southeastern corner of the state. The Historic Route 66 Highway signs turned from blue to brown.

I stopped for lunch at a restored vintage 66 gas station-turned-café that had the actual rusted-brown truck that inspired the

184

character Tow Mater in *Cars.*

I wasn't alone in the café. Somehow I had caught up to the Corvette-driving Canadians I'd run into at the Munger Moss Motel. We had a burger together along with two Australians who had started their trek in Los Angeles and were following the Route from west to east.

One of the Canadians was complaining about the difficulty of following the Route along some stretches, and the Australian erupted, "You think you got it hard, mate? Half the cities don't even have signs facing west. You have to drive the bloody thing with one eye in the rearview mirror!"

CHAPTER TWENTY-FIVE

THERE ARE PEOPLE WHO ARE AS MUCH A PART OF THE ROUTE AS THE ROAD ITSELF.
— CHARLES JAMES'S DIARY

Later that afternoon I crossed the border into Oklahoma, the fourth state on Route 66.

The first town I passed warranting a side tour was Commerce, home to baseball great Mickey Mantle (hence the nickname "the Commerce Comet"). I took a slight detour to walk by his boyhood home. There were still dents on the garage door where the young Mantle used to throw baseballs.

I stopped nearby for an ice cream cone at a Dairy King built in a restored 1927 gas station — probably the fifth or sixth Route 66–era gas station I'd encountered since starting my trek. The owner told me with obvious pride that the gangsters Bonnie and

Clyde were fond of Commerce since Bonnie had cousins in town and, if chased, they could get over several state borders quickly. Back then, police didn't have radios and legally couldn't cross the state line even when chasing a known public enemy.

The towns sported names like Narcissa, Afton, Vinita, Chelsea, and Catoosa with its famous blue whale — a consummate Route 66 attraction.

The whale was built in the 1970s by a zoologist named Hugh Davis, who erected the edifice for his wife to add to her collection of whale figurines. The blue whale is twenty feet tall and eighty feet long, and was constructed over the course of two years with cement that was mixed and applied one bucket at a time. I was thinking about what an absurd thing this man had done for his woman, and then I remembered what I was doing for mine.

The walking was easy and mostly pleasant until I reached Tulsa, where the Route got confusing as the highway is marked 66 but isn't *the* Route 66. It was just as well, as the freeway was too busy to walk on anyway.

Tulsa's a nice town, I had held successful seminars there before, but I didn't stop. I was eager to reach Oklahoma City and the Texas border.

Three days west of Tulsa I walked through Stroud, a small town with beautiful old homes and the famous Rock Café, owned by Sally, the namesake of the lead female character from *Cars*. The restaurant's walls displayed notes and sketchings from John Lasseter and the Pixar artists who came through Stroud to be inspired and apparently fell for the place, as well as the restaurant's proprietor.

Later that same day, I stopped by another iconic Route 66 site, McJerry's Route 66 Gallery. Jerry McClanahan was the illustrator and creator of the Route 66 guide and maps I had purchased back in Joliet and had been using since.

It was interesting to meet the man behind the words I'd been following. Jerry was in no hurry to be anywhere, so we ended up spending several hours talking about the Route as he shared anecdotes of the people who had stopped by his place — the famous and infamous.

By the time we finished talking it was getting dark, so I ended up having dinner with Jerry back at the Rock Café.

The next four days were more small towns as I passed the Route 66 Rock of Ages Farm, a miniature replica of the blue whale of Catoosa (as if one weren't enough), the famous "1898 Round Barn" in Arcadia, and one of my favorite stops — POPS, the ultimate soda gallery with a sixty-six-foot soda bottle out front and more than seven hundred different flavors of soda, including Coffee, Cucumber, Bacon, Peanut Butter, Buffalo Wing, and the classics Bug Barf and Gus's Pimple Pop.

Putting my curiosity aside, I had a cheeseburger and fries with a relatively safe Peruvian Inka Kola, which tasted a little like bubble gum. Two days later I reached Oklahoma City.

CHAPTER TWENTY-SIX

SOME PERSONALITIES ARE TOO LARGE TO BE CONTAINED IN A SMALL LOCALE.
— CHARLES JAMES'S DIARY

I entered Oklahoma City on the one-and-a-half-month anniversary of starting my walk. I still hadn't reached the Route's halfway point, which was still about three hundred miles west in Adrian, Texas, but it was an important landmark all the same.

It was an uneventful day, though it was difficult to follow the Route. There were a lot of turns and new roads, and I was grateful that I had my guidebook and map or I probably would have ended up in some other county.

I spent the night in downtown Oklahoma City and got up early the next morning to get back out on the road, stopping at a

Waffle House for breakfast shortly after sunrise.

There's a unique society that exists in all pancake and waffle houses, one unabashedly provincial and real, like something drawn from a Steinbeck novel. As I was waiting to give my order, I heard this conversation between an old man and a waitress.

"Morning, Dawn."

"Morning, Albert. I already know what you're going to order. Biscuits and gravy."

"Well, now, Dawn. I might just surprise you today and order the steak and eggs."

"What. You win the lottery?"

The next week and a half was a blur. I passed Yukon, hometown of country singer Garth Brooks, then El Reno, which on its city sign proclaims itself the home of the 750-pound onion burger. Every year, a massive hamburger is made then paraded through town so everyone can have a bite. I wondered where they got a bun that size.

From El Reno I walked through Calumet, Geary, Bridgeport, Hydro, Weatherford, and Clinton. These communities were all small slices of Americana — the kind of towns where people paint the American flag on the side of their garage and barn, and old men come out of their houses as you walk by just to wave to you. Most of these small towns had once prospered and grown fat off the mother road and have been dying ever since, their survival indelibly linked to the road's health.

Before leaving Clinton I stopped to visit the Route 66 museum. A restored 1937 Ford Highway Patrol car sat in the museum's lobby in front of a large, wall-sized map of Route 66. Along one wall were faded black-and-white photographs of the workers building the road and pictures of Okies, headed west in jalopies piled high with all their belongings.

I overheard a tour guide say to a group, "People say Route 66 is getting too commercial, but let's face it, it's always been commercial. Route 66 was created to turn a buck."

I wondered what Ramona at the Munger Moss Motel would have to say about that.

I also heard him say, with thinly veiled anger, "It was President Eisenhower who killed 66 with his signing of the Federal Highway Act of 1956 and the birth of the interstate highway system." He made Eisenhower sound like he'd murdered the road.

I left the museum, walking past the Trade Winds Motel, where my guidebook said that Elvis stayed often, always in room 215. Apparently Elvis was a creature of habit.

My next stop, Elk City, had another Route 66 museum with the largest Route 66 shield I'd passed so far, towering maybe thirty feet in the air. The museum had an Old West town, a massive collection of weather vanes, and a ranch equipment exhibit. I visited the museum, then took a rest day to do my laundry before heading back out on the road.

The next two days I walked through Sayre and Erick, both small, "blink-and-you'll-miss-'em" towns. Erick did produce two famous citizens, though both were nearly as old as the Route itself and now nearly as forgotten.

The first was Sheb Wooley, who was an actor in the western classic *High Noon* and, oddly enough, wrote the song "Purple People Eater," which sat at number one on the *Billboard* charts for five weeks in 1958.

The second Erick celebrity was Roger Miller, the musician who sang the trucker classic "King of the Road." The lyrics stuck in my head. "I'm a man of means by no means, king of the road." My dad liked that song. He'd sing along with the radio every time it played.

The next morning I reached the town of Texola — so named because it's in both

Texas and Oklahoma — and crossed the border into the Lone Star State. State number five.

CHAPTER TWENTY-SEVEN

I ONCE, FROM THE STAGE, CLAIMED TO PUT THE STAR IN THE LONE STAR STATE. NOW I'M JUST THE LONE.
— CHARLES JAMES'S DIARY

Texas is the largest of the Route 66 states but has the second-shortest stretch of the Route's road, as 66 only passes through the Texas panhandle.

By nightfall I reached Shamrock, an Irish settlement with a population of under two thousand. Every year all the men in town grow beards for Saint Patrick's Day, putting a price on the head of any adult male not sporting one.

I stayed at the aptly named Blarney Inn, which advertised itself as "A Wee Bit of Ireland Here in Shamrock." The young man at the hotel counter told me that an actual fragment of the famed Blarney stone was in a park just a few miles away. "You should go see it," he said. "If you kiss it, you'll become eloquent."

I just thanked him and took my room key. I thought if I had a car, I would probably go see it, but five miles of walking to see a stone isn't worth it. And I was eloquent enough. Not that it was going to do me much good out here.

On my way out of Shamrock the next morning, I walked past one of the most interesting displays of Route 66 architecture, the U-Drop Inn, a gift shop, restaurant, and information center. The beautiful building, which looks totally out of place in the dusty town, is an art deco masterpiece and the inspiration for Ramone's House of Body Art in the movie *Cars*.

By late afternoon I reached McLean. The most interesting thing about the small town (actually the *only* interesting thing about the small town) was that it was once a World War II German POW camp. I had no idea that German prisoners were ever kept on US soil. There was a war museum but it was terribly disappointing, looking more like a poorly stocked Army-Navy supply shop than a museum.

I spent the night at McLean's Cactus Inn. If I had known what the next day would bring, I would have just stayed in bed. I should have stayed in bed. It was another one of those life-changing what-if moments. Only this time I was on the wrong side of it.

CHAPTER TWENTY-EIGHT

**THE WOMAN AT THE HOTEL
WARNED ME TO WATCH OUT
FOR SNAKES. SHE DIDN'T
SPECIFY THE KIND WITH FEET.
— CHARLES JAMES'S DIARY**

The next morning at breakfast, Dana, the hotel's proprietor, informed me that there was no place to stay between McLean and Conway, which was a little less than fifty miles — at least two days' walking. I wasn't overly concerned. The weather was warm, and I told her that I could sleep outside in my sleeping bag and tent. She warned me to watch out for striped bark scorpions and diamondback rattlesnakes.

I filled my canteen and water bottles, then set off for the day. There was little to see but miles of dusty earth. I passed an old 66 gas station that was vandalized and deteriorating, as its whereabouts created no incen-

198

tive for anyone to restore it or to tear it down.

At around two in the afternoon I passed the Donley County, Texas, Route 66 Safety Rest Area, Museum, and Tornado Shelter. In spite of having the longest name of any government building in the free world, the facility was nicely built and featured modern eating pavilions and a large children's playground.

The fact that the government had felt the need to build a shelter out here made me wonder how often they got tornadoes in the area. I had no desire to see one. One thing was for sure — in this terminally flat landscape, you would see it coming long before it swallowed you.

The sun was an orange ball touching the horizon in front of me when I decided to camp for the night. It wasn't an ideal campsite, exposed without trees or foliage, but no worse than anywhere else I could see.

I walked about fifty yards from the highway, made a cursory search for snakes and scorpions, then set up my tent.

It was about an hour after I'd made camp when I heard the nonmuffled roar of a motorcycle, followed by a chorus of others. The sound of the engines slowed, as if they were braking. I looked out of my tent and watched the motorcycles U-turn on the highway and head back in my direction. I could think of no reason they would turn around in the middle of nowhere except one.

I thought of going for my gun, but there were more than a few problems with that. First, my gun was locked in the bottom of my pack and was unloaded. Second, there were at least four of them, and if they were as bad as they looked, they were likely armed.

And third, they were already on me, the bikes' headlamps bouncing around me as they rode off-road over the rugged terrain.

I stood at their arrival. The first motorcycle pulled up within a few yards from me. I knew nothing of motorcycle gang protocol, but I guessed the bike's rider to be their leader. He was older than me, barrel-chested and bald with a frayed, reddish-gray beard that fell below his tattoo-inked neck. His scalp and face were also tattooed, and there were four teardrops below his right eye.

Growing up in a poor part of Ogden, Utah, my best friend had two brothers in a gang. I knew enough about that tattoo to know what it meant — one mock tear for every man he'd killed. I couldn't believe I had escaped a plane crash only to be killed ignominiously by a motorcycle gang. Given the choice, I think I would have taken the plane crash. It was less personal.

The four cyclists cut their engines, leaving the air suddenly and painfully quiet. With the exception of the lead rider, it was difficult to see the other men's faces with the cycles' headlamps facing me.

"What are you doing here?" the leader asked.

"I'm just camping."

"This is our desert."

"I didn't know," I said. "It looked like public property."

"Shut up." He looked down at my pack, which was leaning against the outside of my tent. He said to the large man at his right, "Check that."

The rider leaned his bike on its stand and got off. He was even bigger than he looked on the bike. He wore a black vest almost completely covered with a collage of patches. He walked over and lifted my pack, unzipped the top of it, turned it upside down, and shook it. Everything fell out in a pile, including my gun, diary, and phone. The tall man rooted through the pile, put my phone in his pocket, and lifted the gun.

"He's got this."

"Give it to me," the leader said. The man handed it over. The leader examined it, then looked back at me. "Why do you have a piece?"

"It can be dangerous out here." I think he missed my intended irony.

He checked its magazine, then put the gun in his vest.

"What else he got? Go through the pack."

I was afraid he would say that. The man dug through the pockets and pulled out the vinyl bank pouch I kept my money in. He unzipped it. "Look at this." He tossed the pouch to the leader.

The man looked inside the pouch, ran his fingers through the bills, then zipped it back up, shoved it under his vest, and looked at me. "Why do you have so much cash?"

"I'm walking to California."

"You sell drugs?"

"No."

"You have drugs?"

"No."

"Why do you have so much cash?"

"I'm walking to California."

"Where are you going?"

"LA. I'm going to see my wife and kid."

"Give me your wallet."

I took it out of my pocket and handed it

to him. As he looked through it, I said, "Can I keep my driver's license? It's no use to you." Then I added, "You're not going to want to be caught with it."

"I'm not going to get caught with any-thing." He took out my credit cards and cash, then tossed the wallet back to me with the license intact.

"Thank you," I said.

"He's got a watch," the large guy said.

"Give me your watch."

My Rolex. Then I remembered that I had Monica's ring. I knew he would demand it if he found it. I also knew I wouldn't give it to him. He would have to take it. I decided to distract him instead.

I slowly took off my watch, stepped for-ward, and handed it to him — actually, I presented it to him as if he were a customer in the Rolex boutique on New York's Fifth Avenue. "Congratulations. It's a Rolex."

He studied the watch, then looked back up at me. "Is it real?"

"It's real. It's worth more than fifty grand."

"Why do you have so much money?"

"I used to be rich."

"Why used to be? What happened?"

"I quit my job."

"Why?"

"I hated my boss."

The leader grinned. "What else he got?"

The big guy tossed my things around some more, then said, "That's it."

"Just take the whole pack," one of the men behind him said.

"I don't need a pack."

The leader looked at me. "What else you got in there?"

"Clothes. Deodorant. Maps. You have everything of value."

He glanced over at the big guy and nodded. He walked back to his cycle.

"You can sleep in our desert tonight," he said. He started his bike, revved his motor, then spun his bike around, kicking up dirt and rocks around me. The others followed. I couldn't make out the "motorcycle club's" name on the back of their vests. I stood there, watching their taillights disappear into the distance. Just like that, everything I had was gone. At least they hadn't killed me.

Chapter Twenty-Nine

Small Gifts Shine Bright
in the Darkness of Want.
— Charles James's Diary

As calm as I'd acted, or thought I had, I was pretty shaken up. It took me a while to even lie down, and then I couldn't sleep. I just lay there, listening to the sounds of the desert and the occasional passing vehicle. Around two or three in the morning, a pack of coyotes began howling.

Finally, I got up before the sun, rolled up my tent, and started walking. My pack was noticeably lighter, but my step was measurably heavier. I reached the town of Groom by ten a.m. I had no money. No credit cards. Nothing but some camping equipment and hunger.

Near the road was a restaurant with an odd name, *The Grill — Welcome Home.* I walked in. The place was surprisingly nice for a diner in the middle of nowhere. There was only one other man in the diner.

A waitress walked up to me. She was about my age, with dishwater-blond hair and pretty but weary-looking eyes. She wore a sheer white blouse with a silver cross falling above her cleavage.

"Just you today?" she asked.

"Yes."

She started to turn but I stopped her. "Hold on a second; I need to tell you something."

She looked at me expectantly.

"I'm hungry, but I can't pay. I mean, I can pay you back. I just don't have any money on me."

She looked at me for a moment, then said, "Well, that was honest."

"I was robbed last night by a motorcycle gang."

Her expression changed. "A motorcycle gang?"

I nodded. "Yes, ma'am."

She said, "Four guys, their leader was bald with a long red beard? Had teardrop tattoos?"

For a moment I wondered if they were friends of hers. "You know them?"

"No. They stopped here for dinner last night. They had a lot of money in a bag."

"A dark-blue bank bag with a zipper?"

She nodded. "Yeah. It was full of cash. Big bills."

"That was mine."

She frowned. "I'm sorry." Then she said, "I'll be right back." She walked back into the kitchen and returned a moment later. "Here." She handed me a hundred-dollar bill.

"What's this?"

"They left me a hundred-dollar tip."

"You're giving it to me?"

"It's your money," she said.

I looked at the bill, surprised by the gesture. "Most people wouldn't do that."

"How do you know?"

Her reply stumped me. "I guess I don't." I looked around. "Is there a bank around here?"

"Not here. There's one in Conway. It's not far. About fifteen miles."

"I'm on foot."

"Then it's far."

I sighed a little. "Could I get some coffee? Now that I have money?"

"Don't worry about it. I'll buy you some breakfast. I think you could use it." She led me to a table in the corner of the room and handed me a menu.

"What's your name?" I asked.

"Brenda."

"Brenda what?"

"Benson."

"I have a friend with that last name," I said. It was the first time I'd called McKay a friend since I'd left him.

"Are you from here?"

"Groom?" she said. "No one is from Groom. They just get stuck here."

"Thank you again," I said.

"You're welcome." She filled my coffee, then walked away. When she returned with my breakfast, I said, "May I ask you something?"

"Sure."

"Can you sit down?"

She glanced back at the door, then said, "Sure." She sat down at the table across from me. "Ask away."

"Why did you help me?"

She looked at me quizzically, as if I'd asked her a trick question. "Because you needed help."

"That might be the most perfect answer ever given to that question."

She shrugged a little. "What other answer is there?"

"So tell me, how did Brenda Benson get stuck in Groom, Texas?"

"You mean that's not every little girl's

dream, to be a poor waitress in a dying town in the middle of nowhere?"

I grinned. "I don't think so."

She sighed heavily. "I came here with my boyfriend when he got a job in Amarillo. Turns out he had other interests, if you know what I mean. Then I got pregnant, and he vanished. I was relying on him for money. That's how I got stuck here."

"No family back home?"

"No family. No home."

"That hundred dollars you gave back was a big deal, wasn't it?"

"It was your money."

"But if it wasn't . . ."

"It would have helped pay some bills."

"I thought so," I said. "So tell me something. If you could go someplace else, where would it be?"

She laughed. "Anyplace away from here."

"I'm serious."

She cocked her head. "You're going to make my dreams come true?"

"Maybe."

She laughed again. "Okay, I'll play along. I always wanted to go to Venice. Fall in love with a handsome Italian guy."

"So you're a dreamer. I don't know about the Italian guy, but the rest is doable."

She shook her head. "It's a nice fiction.

What's your name?"

"Charles. Charles James."

"Where are you going, Charles?"

"I'm walking Route 66. I started in Chicago and I'm walking to LA."

"You're almost halfway," she said. "Why are you walking?"

"Call it a pilgrimage."

"Okay, Pilgrim." She turned back as an older couple walked in. "I better get back to work before Steve starts yelling at me."

"Wait, one more thing," I said. "What would you say if I told you that I was really a multimillionaire who could make your dreams come true?"

She looked at me for a moment, then said, "I'd say you're a bigger dreamer than I am." She stood. "Enjoy your breakfast."

I finished eating, filled my water bottles with ice water from the restaurant's pitchers, and then got up to go. I waited until Brenda came back out from the kitchen to thank her.

"Are you going to report the crime?" she asked.

"No."

She nodded as if she understood. "I doubt it would do any good. Be careful out there."

It took me four and a half hours to reach the town of Conway. It was three in the afternoon when I walked into the bank. My shirt was stained with sweat as I approached the teller. She looked at me uneasily.

I took out my driver's license. "Hi. I need to transfer some money and get some cash. Could you help me?"

"Do you have a bank order?"

"I have my account number. I'll have to log in on a computer. It's an offshore account in the Cayman Islands."

The woman looked at me skeptically.

"I know I don't look like I have anything, but I actually have a lot of money. I got robbed last night, just outside of McLean. I just need a computer to wire the money over."

She hesitated a moment, then said, "All right. Come over here."

I followed her over to a cubicle, and she sat down in front of a computer. "Your account?"

Only then did I remember that my account numbers were on my smartphone. I had backups on my computer at home, but that was a world away.

"Your account?" the woman repeated.

"I don't know it," I said, raking my hand back through my hair. "The numbers were on my phone. They stole that too."

She paused. For the first time she looked

like she might believe me. "Is there someone you can call?"

I breathed out slowly. "No. There isn't." I shook my head, then stood, my head spinning at the reality of my situation. "I'm sorry to waste your time." I grabbed my pack and walked out of the bank. By the grace of a poor waitress, I had a hundred dollars to live on, but besides that I had no way, without coming out, to get any more money.

I stopped at the grocery store and, breaking my hundred-dollar bill, bought a loaf of bread and a jar of peanut butter. I grabbed a plastic knife from their deli, refilled my water bottles from a drinking fountain, and then went out behind the store to a soft patch of grass and laid down against my pack. I was stuck. My trek was doomed. And I hadn't even made it halfway to Santa Monica and my Monica.

CHAPTER THIRTY

MY ROAD HAS TAKEN AN UNEXPECTED DETOUR.
— CHARLES JAMES'S DIARY

The next morning I started walking before sunrise, as much to avoid humanity as the sun. Without a watch I wasn't really sure what time it was, but I suspected that it was around four a.m.

I knew that I wasn't far from Amarillo, which might now be the last city on my walk. The thought angered me. I couldn't believe that I had come this far only to fail.

An hour later, as I entered the Amarillo city limits, I could make out a group of a dozen or more people congregated under a streetlamp next to the curb of a 7-Eleven.

With the exception of an occasional truck driver, I had seen no one that morning, so a group of people just standing in the street looked almost surreal; like a mirage.

As I got closer, I could see that the people were all Hispanic. I counted about a dozen men and three women. I guessed they were migrant workers, waiting to be picked up by a local farm.

I felt a kinship with these people. Not just because they were most likely Mexican like me but because they were pickers and toilers. They were *my* people. My paternal great-grandfather was a Mexican sharecropper, my grandfather was a migrant worker, and even if my father had run from migrant work, he had still spent his life working the ground. Even I had for a time.

I had one other thing in common with them. I needed money.

One of the men looked up at me as I approached. *"Buenos días, amigo."*

"Días or *noches?"*

He grinned. "You looking for work, *amigo?"* He spoke English with only a slight accent. The rest of the group looked at us.

"Maybe. Where's work?"

"In Plainview."

"Where's Plainview?"

"It is about an hour from here. The farm trucks will pick us up soon."

"What does it pay?" I asked, walking closer.

The man was near my age, with thick

black hair. He wore a dirty long-sleeved shirt.

"Eight dollars an hour and a place to stay."

Eight dollars an hour. Working the stage, I'd make more than eight dollars a *second* on a bad day. Actually, double that. But I wasn't on the stage anymore.

"You speak good English."

"So do you."

"What's your name?" I asked.

"Eddie."

I extended my hand. "Nice to meet you, Eddie." We shook.

Just then two Ford pickup trucks, one white, one metallic black, pulled up alongside the curb. I knew the kind of trucks they were because I was with McKay when he purchased one to pull his boat. Ford F-450 Crew Cab. They cost more than most luxury cars. McKay's cost nearly eighty thousand.

A tall, well-fed man got out of the driver's side of the second truck, dully eyeing us. He shouted, "C'mon, move it." He let down his truck's tailgate, then walked to the other truck and let down its tailgate as well.

There was room inside the double cab for at least four more, but I didn't expect that the people behind the tinted glass would be inviting anyone in.

"Let's go," Eddie said to me. He climbed into the bed of the second truck, moving all the way to the front against the cab. He looked back at me. "Are you coming, *amigo?*"

I looked at him for a moment. "Sure. Why not?" I walked over, put my pack in, and climbed in after it.

The farmer shut the tailgate and got back into his truck. He honked, and both trucks pulled out into the road.

I looked around at my new associates. There were eight of us. Everyone sat quietly, most with their heads down to catch some sleep, their hair fluttering in the cool Texas air. Their hard, dark faces bore the strain of ten thousand hours under the sun.

We sat close, our bodies pressed together, not because the bed was crowded but because it was cold. In spite of Texas's infamous summer heat, it still dropped into the low sixties at night and with the wind chill factor, it felt more like fifty.

"What's your name?" Eddie asked, fiddling with the zipper on his jacket.

"Charles."

"Charles. That is a gringo name. What is your last name?"

I almost said *James* but stopped myself. "Gonzales."

"Gonzales. That is one of our names."

"Have you been to Plainview before?" I asked.

"Yes. I came last year too."

"What are we harvesting?" I asked.

"We are not harvesting. We are pulling weeds."

"Why don't they just use weed spray?"

"That is what they want to do. It is cheaper. But this is a new kind of weed. It has grown too strong for the poison they give it. Now they must pull it by hand."

"A genetic mutation," I said.

He looked at me blankly, then went back to fiddling with his coat zipper. After a few more unsuccessful tries at repairing it he looked back up at me. "Where are you coming from?"

"Chicago."

"You hitchhiked from Chicago?"

"I walked."

He studied me as if he were deciding whether I was telling the truth or not. "That is a long walk, gringo. Where are you walking to?"

"California."

"There is much work in California. Much to harvest."

"That's what I'm hoping," I said.

CHAPTER THIRTY-ONE

THERE ARE TOO MANY SELF-PROCLAIMED "SOCIAL WARRIORS" WHOSE PRIMARY REASON FOR RAISING THEIR HAND IS NOT TO LIFT THE POOR BUT TO STRIKE THE RICH.
— CHARLES JAMES'S DIARY

Plainview, Texas, was about seventy-five miles directly south of Amarillo. As we approached the town, I spotted a municipal water tower that read, "Welcome to Rustwater."

I turned to Eddie. "I thought we were going to Plainview."

"This is Plainview," Eddie said.

"Why does the water tower say 'Rustwater'?"

"Many years ago they made a movie here. The movie people painted the water tower for the movie, but they never painted it back."

The sky had turned a slightly paler shade of twilight as we passed the PLAINVIEW city sign with its accompanying Rotary and Lions club monikers. A mile later the truck pulled up to a convenience store.

"What are we doing?" I asked.

"We buy food and drinks," Eddie said.

The store was already crowded with migrant workers, most buying coffee and energy drinks — liquid energy to get them through the day. I bought a couple of sodas, a peanut candy bar, and a bag of jerky, then returned to the truck. I think that I was still in disbelief that I'd even come.

Eddie came out a few minutes after me carrying two large bags of groceries. Sitting in the pickup bed, he brought out a bag of *chicharrones* — fried pig rinds. He opened the bag, releasing a pungent odor. He put one in his mouth and crunched loudly, then tilted the bag forward to offer me some.

"My dad used to eat these," I said, taking a rind.

"They are good for you," Eddie said. "They are *muy* protein."

Eddie ate a few more, then said, "Gringo, do you know a famous person is from Plainview?"

"No," I said. "Who?"

"Jimmy Dean."

"You mean James Dean, the actor?"

He shook his head. "Jimmy Dean."

"You mean, the guy who makes sausage?"

"Yes."

I laughed. "How do you know who Jimmy Dean is?"

"I like his sausage."

The driver of our truck honked and several men frantically came running out of the store and climbed back in the trucks. The trucks pulled back out onto the road.

A few minutes later we drove by a darkened metal warehouse that looked to have been turned into a restaurant. A large hand-painted sign with Christmas lights around the border read Taqueria Perlita's.

"Perlita's," Eddie said, nodding approvingly. "Her tamales and chili verde is *muy bueno.*"

"That's really her name?"

"*Sí.* Maybe after we make some money we will go there for dinner."

The farm and its two thousand acres of cotton fields were about ten minutes from our grocery stop. Our trucks pulled up alongside two others, perpendicular to the fledgling cotton plants. The same man who had herded us into the trucks in Amarillo jumped out of the truck and shouted, "Everybody out," even though most of the workers were already on the ground. No one bothered to drop the tailgates but jumped down over the sides of the trucks onto the rutted dirt.

"I can leave my pack here?" I asked.

"Sí."

I followed Eddie as the group moved toward a short man holding a notepad. The man wore a light, fluorescent yellow-green vinyl vest that made him look like a crossing guard. He had a cigarette clamped between his front teeth.

"Where are we going?" I asked Eddie.

"We must sign in with the crew leader. That is how we get paid. You have not done this before?"

"No."

He grinned. "I hope it does not kill you, gringo."

The sun was just beginning to emerge above the cotton as the workers formed a line in front of the crew leader. The man was white with reddish auburn hair and sunburned cheeks. When it was my turn, I stepped up to him. He had a badge that read CURTIS. I didn't know if it was a first or last name. I had a feeling it didn't matter. He looked me over and, blowing out a puff of smoke through clenched teeth, put his pen to his sheet. *"Cómo te llamas?"*

"My name is Charles Gonzales," I answered.

He looked up at me. "You speak English."

"I'm American," I said.

"Congratulations," he said snidely. "You pulled pigweed before?"

"I used to be in landscape architecture."

He chortled. "We got us a Frank Lloyd Wright," he said, shaking his head with derision. "Landscape architecture. You pulled pigweed or not?"

"No."

"It ain't rocket science. Some of the roots, you're gonna have to hoe 'em out. Then put 'em in bags. Don't shake the plant. The seeds spread. That's why we burn 'em." He wrote my name down on his list. *"Frank Gonzales."* I wasn't sure whether he'd actually mixed up my name or he was still mocking me for my landscape-architecture comment. "Pay is eight dollars an hour. We pay at the end of each shift. Grab a hoe and some bags and get to work." As I turned away from him I heard him mutter, "Landscape architecture."

I walked over to the edge of the field where Eddie was waiting for me with two hoes and a pair of yellow faux-leather gloves. We walked out into the tilled soil of the cotton field. The cotton plants were not yet waist high and the viral weed had all but taken them over. I attempted to pull a weed by hand and realized this was going to be a lot tougher than I'd realized.

"Use the hoe," Eddie said.

"So you pulled this before?"

"Yes. Last year. This pigweed was not a problem when I first came to America. Now it is a big problem. It is everywhere."

I dug my hoe into the baked earth and, pulling as hard as I could, tore out a weed.

Just then the crew leader shouted at me. "Move it, Frank."

Eddie didn't look up from his hoe but said, "Why does he call you Frank?"

"He thinks he's funny." I glanced over; Curtis was still staring at me. "Is he going to watch us all day?"

"That is his job."

Curtis shouted, "Keep it movin', Frank."

I dug faster. "I feel like a slave."

"Yes," Eddie said. "Maybe."

A few minutes later Eddie said, "You know, gringo, you can eat this weed. It is very good for you. And it grows very good, even in drought. People have eaten it for thousands of years in Mexico."

"Maybe they should grow these instead of

cotton. It seems to grow better."

"That would be too smart, gringo."

Chapter Thirty-Two

ACCORDING TO THE ARTICLE I
READ, PIGWEED, A PRODUCT OF
EVOLUTION, HAS BEEN SPREADING
THROUGHOUT THE SOUTHERN PART
OF THE US FOR NEARLY A DECADE
NOW. NO PESTICIDE KILLS IT THAT
WON'T KILL THE CROP AS WELL.
LEFT ALONE, IT GROWS UPWARD OF
SEVEN FEET HIGH, AND IS TOUGH
ENOUGH TO DAMAGE FARM
EQUIPMENT. I GUESS THAT MAKES
ME A SOLDIER IN THE BATTLE
AGAINST THE PERFECT WEED.
— CHARLES JAMES'S DIARY

If it hadn't been for my three weeks of walking and the strength I'd gained from it, I wouldn't have made it through the first day. Probably not even the first hour. Curtis must have smelled weakness on me; he kept after me all day. Sometimes warranted, sometimes not. It took all the restraint I could muster not to throttle him.

In addition to the difficulty of the work, the sun was merciless, and the whole day I was drenched in sweat.

We stopped around eleven for lunch. My muscles already ached. I couldn't remember the last time that I had worked so hard.

Eddie and I sat down together. He tossed me a handkerchief. "Put that around your neck. Your skin is too fair, gringo. Are you sure you are Mexican?"

I tied the cloth around my neck. "Half. My mother was Irish. White as snow."

"You got her skin, gringo."

I opened my bag and brought out all I had purchased: a candy bar, some jerky, and sodas. Eddie looked at my ration. "That is all you have to eat?"

"Yeah," I said. "I didn't get the memo."

Eddie's brow furrowed. "Memo?"

"I didn't know how this worked. I assumed that they fed us."

He shook his head. "No. Some farms will feed the workers, but they charge a lot of money. It is better this way." He leaned forward and handed me half of his sandwich. "Take this."

As hungry as I was, I didn't take it. "No, it's your lunch."

"I have more. You can buy food tomorrow night. They will drive us to the grocery store."

"You sure?"

"I have more."

I took the sandwich. "Thank you."

The sandwich had cheese, ham, wilted lettuce, and mayo on a hoagie bun. Eddie also had a block of cheddar cheese and a package of tortillas. We broke off pieces of cheese and rolled them in the tortillas. Such simple food had never tasted so good. Twenty minutes later a whistle blew.

"That's it?" I asked.

"Thirty minutes for lunch," Eddie said.

My legs had cramped up as I sat, and I stood with difficulty. I practically hobbled back to the cotton field. *This isn't worth eight dollars an hour,* I thought. *It's not worth eight dollars a minute.*

At around four o'clock, another whistle blew, signaling the end of the workday. We had worked for ten hours, though it felt like more. Outside of my childhood labor, it was the hardest money I'd ever worked for.

A pungent, acrid odor filled the air. About sixty yards from the field, the mountain of weeds we'd picked were burning, giving off thick, black smoke that rose in a column nearly a mile high. Eddie and I carried our bags and hoes over to a truck. I retrieved my pack from the truck we'd come in, and then we walked — in my case, limped — back to where Curtis was standing. There was an armed security guard next to him holding a bag of money. Curtis was going down his list distributing payment. He called a name and someone would step forward and he'd hand them their money.

When he called my pseudonym, "Frank," I stepped up to him. He handed me three twenty-dollar bills. For a moment I just looked at them in my grimy hands, then said, "We worked ten hours."

"Mostly," he said.

"You said we got paid eight dollars an hour."

The foreman's eyes narrowed. "You did. I took twenty for transportation."

"Transportation?"

"You got a ride here, didn't ya?"

"No one said anything about charging us."

"Not my problem," he said. "You don't like it, go find something else. Now get the hell out of here."

In my previous life I would have knocked the man to the ground. Instead, I turned and walked back to where Eddie stood. He shook his head. "It is the way it is, gringo. They take something from everything."

Eddie and I walked over to one of the produce trucks, where most of the workers had already climbed aboard. I pulled myself up onto the truck, though my aching arms nearly gave out.

"Are they going to charge us for this ride too?" I asked.

Eddie nodded. "Yes. Everything."

After twenty minutes or so, the engine started up, shaking the truck with its exertion. Then it lurched forward, tossing us all back into each other like dominoes. One of the men fell off the truck. They left him.

I said to Eddie, "I don't like Legree."

His forehead furrowed. "Who?"

"The crew leader. Simon Legree."

Eddie looked confused. "That is not his name."

"I know."

"I do not understand."

"Simon Legree. He was a plantation owner in *Uncle Tom's Cabin.*"

Eddie just gazed at me.

"It's a book," I said. "A famous book about slavery."

Eddie thought for a moment, then said, "You call him Legree. Maybe that is why he calls you Frank."

The produce trucks dropped us off about two miles from the cotton fields on a barren acre of dirt and weeds adjacent to the far east side of the property. There were eight squat, flat-topped buildings constructed of a weathered gray corrugated metal housing.

Between two of the buildings was a cage-like structure made of iron pipe built over a concrete pad. The sides were covered with fiberboard and the top of the structure had four bars running horizontally across it, a platform for a five-hundred-gallon plastic water tank. A green hose ran from the bottom of the tank and was coiled up on the concrete. This was the community shower. There was no drain. The water just ran off onto the dirt around the pad.

There was an old tractor tire just a few yards from the tower with a wooden door on it piled with blankets. It was somebody's bed.

My quads and lower back were aching as I walked toward the structure. "This is our housing?"

Eddie sensed my disappointment. "It is not so bad, gringo."

I stopped and looked at him. "How is this not bad?"

"Many times I have had worse. One place in Oregon charged us five hundred dollars a month for our housing. Our house, for six of us, was a shipping container with a bucket for a toilet."

"That would be worse," I conceded.

I followed Eddie inside the shack. *Worse, but not by much.* It was a large, open room, paneled with plywood and filled with various-sized beds.

The room had just one window, which was partially veiled with a stained bedsheet for a curtain, darkening the room. I remembered once yelling at the Buckhead Ritz-Carlton's concierge because I didn't like the way my bed had been made. I was a long way from the Ritz.

In the middle of the space a naked lightbulb hung from a rusted steel supporting beam that ran horizontally across the length of the room. The light's cord dangled thirty or forty inches above one of the beds and was held against the wall by a nail that had been pounded into the plywood and then bent around the cord. The line ran down to an uncovered electrical outlet.

The beds were simple box frames with thin, single mattresses covered with grimy, torn covers.

"It ain't five star," I said beneath my breath. I lay my pack on one of the beds, then turned to Eddie. "I think we need to call housekeeping. They forgot to leave truffles on the pillows. Oh wait, they forgot to leave pillows."

"I have had worse," Eddie repeated, as he walked between the beds. He swung the lightbulb to one side, then let it swing as shadows played in the room. "It has a lightbulb that works."

"Not sure that's a plus," I said, still looking around. A cockroach scurried across the floor between my feet. I tried to squash it but missed.

"La cucaracha," Eddie said. "That is good."

I laughed. "You are Pollyanna on steroids. What is good about cockroaches?"

"It means there are not so many rats to eat them."

I looked at him empathetically. "This is how you live?"

"It is not so bad," Eddie said again.

"Aren't there laws for housing?"

"There are laws, but they are your laws, not ours." He looked around to make sure that no one from the farm was around. "These people are *sin papeles.* Without papers. They don't even know there are laws, but it makes no difference. Who are they going to complain to? Most of them do not speak English. And if they complain, they will get sent back to Mexico. We are at their mercy."

"What about the government?"

"They make laws to, what is the word . . . keep people from being mad."

"Appease," I said.

He nodded. "But they do not obey their own laws. Farming is a very big money business. It makes billions of dollars. And if they catch a farmer breaking the law, they do not do anything to him. So it does not matter. Who is going to care about us? We are like that *cucaracha*."

"No. You're not." I again panned the room. "Where's the toilet?"

"It is outside. Everyone shares it."

"It? There's only one toilet?"

He added, "It is enough. Most do not bother with a toilet. They just pee where they are." He headed for the door. "Follow me, gringo. I will show you the toilet. Maybe we will be lucky and there will be toilet paper."

Outside the shack, the orange-red Texas sun touched the western horizon. Even though there were a dozen or so women and children in the camp, a man had stripped naked and was showering beneath the water tank.

I was following Eddie to the outhouse when Legree pulled into camp in an older-model Chevy pickup truck. He parked in front of what looked to be an office building about twenty-five yards from where Eddie and I stood. He shouted to me, "Hey, Frank."

I looked at him.

"Come here. I've got someplace for you."

I turned to Eddie. "Let's go see. Maybe he has someplace better."

"He is not talking to me," Eddie said.

Legree stood there looking at me impatiently. "Haven't got all day."

I walked over to him, and he led me inside the building. It was a large, open room with fluorescent lighting. It had once been an office of sorts but now it was mostly used as storage; it was piled with old desks and file cabinets, assorted junk, like an indoor landfill.

There were three beds in the room, and it appeared that the former occupants had arranged the furniture around the beds to give them privacy. It was definitely an improvement over the hovel Eddie had showed me.

"You can sleep in here. It's got a clean toilet, decent bed."

I looked at him. "Why are you putting me in here?"

"You're different from the others."

At first I was baffled by his offer. I was pretty sure that this guy hated me, so why was he giving me a prime spot? Then I remembered what Eddie had just said. I spoke English and I wasn't an undocumented laborer. If I complained, someone might actually listen. I looked at him for a moment, then shook my head. "I'm no different." I walked back to the shack and my only friend.

CHAPTER THIRTY-THREE

I'VE RECEIVED MORE GENUINE GENEROSITY FROM THIS HUMBLE MAN IN A WEEK THAN I HAVE FROM MY MILLIONAIRE ASSOCIATES IN AN ENTIRE CAREER. PERHAPS TO WANT IS TO UNDERSTAND WANT IN OTHERS.
— CHARLES JAMES'S DIARY

When I returned to the shack, two other men and a woman were there. The woman, who looked at least ten years older than me, eyed me warily.

"Do you know these people?" I asked Eddie.

"Yes. That is Albert, Johnnie, and Eleena."

They each nodded at the sound of their name.

"*Mucho gusto,*" I said to them. They just stared at me. "*Mi casa es su casa?*" Nothing. I turned back to Eddie. "Tough crowd."

236

"They do not know you. We only stay with people we know. We have no place to hide our money."

"Maybe you should ask for a check."

"That is not how it is done. The farmer does not want to make a check. And if they give us a check, who will cash them? Just the payday loan places, but they will charge us a lot of money to cash them, even though they know the farmer and they know that it is a good check." Eddie shook his head. "What did Mr. Legree want?"

I grinned at his adoption of the nickname. "He showed me another place to stay."

"It was good?"

"No. Not as good. Where do I sleep?"

"That bed is for you."

I looked at it. The mattress was depressed in the middle but it was possible that they had given me the best one. "Thank you. *Muchas gracias.*"

They all nodded in acceptance of my thanks.

I opened my pack and laid my pad across the bed along with my sleeping bag. I unzipped my bag and spread it open across the bed like a sheet.

Eddie sat down on the bed across from me, the one with the lightbulb hanging above it, and lay back on the mattress, rubbing his forehead. The mattress squeaked.

"Going to bed so soon?" I asked.

"*Acostarse con las gallinas,* gringo. Morning comes early."

"Right." I lay down as well, taking my journal out of my bag. "Can we leave the light on for a moment? I need to write."

"*Sí.*"

I wrote for about ten minutes, then returned my journal to my pack. "Okay."

Eddie reached up and turned off the light. "*Buenas noches,* gringo."

"*Buenas noches,* Eddie." As I lay there staring at the ceiling, all I could think was, *What have I gotten myself into?*

CHAPTER THIRTY-FOUR

**SLAVERY STILL EXISTS. IT'S JUST BEEN REBRANDED INTO SOMETHING MORE IGNORABLE.
— CHARLES JAMES'S DIARY**

Just as Eddie had warned, morning came early — far too early. In spite of my exhaustion, I hadn't slept very well, tossing and turning on the thin, uneven mattress. I also heard the scurrying of rodents throughout the night. Or maybe they were just monster cockroaches.

I woke to the smell of coffee beans. It was still dark inside our room except for the red glow of a hot plate. I sat up, my neck sunburned and my back aching, likely as much from the bed as the previous day's labor.

Eddie was in the corner of the room squatting down next to the hot plate. The two men and the woman were sitting on the ground next to him. I was the only one still in bed.

On one of the burners was a pot of coffee. On the other Eddie was cooking eggs in a saucepan. To one side of the hot plate, on a torn piece of cardboard box, was a stack of fried corn tortillas. There was a bowl of refried beans on the other.

"Buenos días," Eddie said.

I rubbed my eyes. *"Buenos días."*

"I was about to wake you. It is almost time to work. Come and eat."

I took some money out of my pocket. "I'll pay for this."

"Do not worry. You can buy food tonight."

About half an hour later, I heard the clattering approach of the produce truck, followed by a horn blast. Everyone emerged from their shacks and climbed onto the truck for the two-mile ride back to the cotton fields.

Our group had worked more than a hundred acres the day before, so our gathering point had moved about a quarter mile west. Again, Legree was there to check us in. He looked at me spitefully, likely because I had rejected his offer the night before. Without comment, he wrote down my name. Then he looked up and said, "Let's see if you can earn your wage today."

The weather was better than it had been the day before. It was still uncomfortably hot, but at least there were clouds that offered some relief from the Texas sun. The weeds, unfortunately, were just as stubborn. Even though I was sore, I worked faster than the day before, not that Legree noticed. He harassed me most of the morning, and I was grateful when we stopped for lunch, which Eddie and I took alone. Again, Eddie provided my meal: two tamales wrapped in corn husks and an apple.

"Tonight we go shopping for more groceries," Eddie said. "They will drive us in the truck."

"How much will they charge us?"

"Maybe ten dollars each."

"It's only a couple of miles away."

"It is the way it is," Eddie said. "There is nothing we can do. This is not so bad as other places. Some places charge you money without telling you. Some places you owe them money for working for them."

"That's *The Grapes of Wrath*," I said.

"Grapes? Yes, I have picked grapes."

"No, *The Grapes of Wrath*. It's a book by John Steinbeck." I checked his face for recognition. "It's about the Great Depression."

Eddie shook his head. "You read a lot of

241

books, gringo."

"What I meant was, what they're doing, charging the workers more than they make, that's wage slavery. Slavery in America was supposed to end with Lincoln."

Eddie looked at me darkly. For the first time I saw a glint of anger in his eyes. "Slavery in America never ended, gringo. There is still much. I have seen it."

"Where?"

"Two years ago, I met a man from Nicaragua. He came to America like me, looking for work. He went to Florida and one day he was sitting on the curb with other workers and a man came. He said they needed workers. He said they would pay double what the other farms paid, and his mother was their cook, so the food was good. He said there would be a nice place to stay, even if they charged them a little for it. The *nicaragüense* thought *darle la vuelta a la tortilla.*" He looked at me to see if I understood. "You know what that means?"

"No."

"It means to flip the tortilla. This man thought maybe his life had finally changed for the good. He got in the truck.

"The farm was very far away from any city. The place they were to stay was only the back of a truck. There was no bed to

242

sleep on, only the picking bags. They charge him two hundred dollars a week for his house. They charge for everything. To stand under a hose to shower was five dollars.

"The food was not good. Sometimes just old tortillas, but they charge everyone one hundred dollars a week. If they were caught eating the fruit in the field, they would have to pay five dollars for every fruit. Sometimes they just said they saw them eat fruit when they did not and did not pay them for a full day of work.

"No matter how hard this man worked, he could not make enough money to pay the farm back. After a worker was in debt, the farmer would lock him up at night, sometimes with chains. They would tell him that because he owed them money, he was now their property. I think it is no different from the slaves that came to America from Africa."

"Why didn't they just leave?"

Eddie laughed. "You make it sound easy, gringo. It is not so easy. The farms are far away from the city. If they run, they go after them. They beat them up. He said that one man was beaten until he died. They brought his body back and left it near the workers' place so the others would be afraid. He said the birds came and ate the body."

I set down my food. "How did you meet this man?"

"He was working with me in South Carolina. He was brave and he escaped in the night and a car picked him up. He was a lucky one."

"Those people should go to prison."

Eddie nodded. "Yes. They should. But they won't."

CHAPTER THIRTY-FIVE

WHAT A THING IT IS TO BE LOOKED DOWN UPON BY PEOPLE I ONCE WOULD HAVE LOOKED DOWN ON. — CHARLES JAMES'S DIARY

That evening we went to the store. I felt dirty walking inside. Or maybe I just felt dirty because of the way the other shoppers glanced at us and kept their distance — like we were untouchables. I wanted to shout at them, "I could buy and sell you!" I wanted to but I didn't. They would have just thought I was crazy.

I gave sixty of my hard-earned dollars to Eddie so he could buy our food. He knew better than I did what to buy to stretch our money. It was all so bizarre. I had eaten in fancy restaurants where the tab for my meal was at least ten times that. Still, I was glad to not be living off Eddie anymore. I indulged in several treats. I bought a large Dr.

Pepper with ice (there was no ice back at the farm; actually, there was nothing cold), a chocolate bar, a can of almonds, and a six-pack of Dos Equis. I shared the beer with my roommates when we got back to the shack. They were very happy. Truthfully, they were happier than McKay and I were opening a three-thousand-dollar bottle of twenty-year-old Pappy Van Winkle's bourbon.

Over the next week, every day was a replay of the last, although on the third day, someone brought a radio into the field and there was music. It was Mexican music, mariachi stuff with guitars and trumpets, but it was music. It helped pass the time.

There was no day of rest. The workers — at least we migrant workers — worked seven days a week, which made it more difficult to remember what day it was. In the fields, it didn't really matter.

On the seventh day, Eddie and I were eating lunch when he looked at me with a serious expression.

"Gringo, I want to ask you something."

"Yes?"

"Why are you here, gringo?"

"You invited me."

He shook his head. "You are smart. You read many books. You are American. I think there are other things for you to do that are not so hard. Maybe you could make more money. If I had papers, I would look for another job."

"I know," I said. "The thing is, in some ways, I'm like you. I don't have papers."

"What do you mean?"

"It's hard to explain." I looked at him. "I don't know why I said I would work with you when you asked. Maybe it really was just for the money, but I think there's something else. I come from a family of sharecroppers and migrant workers. I think I wanted to understand them. To really see what their life was like."

"You came from a family of migrant workers like us?"

"*Sí.* My great-grandfather was a sharecropper in Oaxaca. My grandfather was a migrant worker. He crossed the border back when it was easy to cross. He picked whatever he could. Potatoes in Idaho. Tomatoes in Florida. Strawberries in California."

"Strawberries," Eddie said, shaking his head. *"La fruta del diablo."* The devil's fruit.

"Why do you call it that?" I asked.

Eddie reached around and touched his back. "It is so low to the ground. By the end of the day, your back is on fire. It is difficult even to walk." He shook his head.

247

"Every crop has its *maldición*. You understand?"

I nodded. "I understand."

"This is dangerous work, *amigo*. We are exposed to the weather. There is poison on the plants. It gets in our skin. There is much sickness. Even if they say there is a doctor, we have no way to go to him. Many times I have a sickness, maybe the flu, but still I have to work. Picking fruit all day with the flu, in the rain, you do not care if you die. Sometimes you hope you do. This is hard work."

"I'm sorry," I said softly. "Do you regret coming to America?"

"No. It is hard, but it is worse where I came from. Much worse."

"Where are you from?"

"Michoacán."

"How long have you been here? In America."

"Three years the first time. Then eight years. I was sent back the first time."

"What made you decide to come?" I asked.

He flinched at the question. Then he took a long breath. "My wife and I had a baby. One day there was a flood in our village. It carried dead animals in our water. Our baby got sick with the diarrhea." His eyes wa-

248

tered. "We could not pay for a doctor, so she died. I could not let that happen again.

"We work for eight dollars an hour. It is not much to you, but in Mexico I worked for maybe sixteen hundred pesos a day. That is only eight dollars a day. It is barely enough to eat. Here we can eat and send money back home and sometimes buy American things.

"We want American things with American names. Like shoes. The Nike shoes are very good. And iPhones. Many come back from America with these things, and we all think they are rich. We make much, much more money, but it is also more expensive here. If we did not eat some of the fruit we pick, we would sometimes starve."

"The farmers let you eat the fruit?"

"Sometimes. If the crew leader is cruel, he will not. He will humiliate you. Maybe he will hit you."

"He can't do that."

"If you are without papers, he can do whatever he wants, gringo. Or he will call immigration and they will take you away. But many are not mean. They understand us. They cannot say we can eat, but they look away and pretend they do not see us eat." He frowned. "But still, there is poison on the plants."

"Do you think Legree is mean or nice?"

Eddie glanced over at him. The crew leader was sitting in his truck drinking a beer. "He is both."

I hadn't seen the "nice" part of him yet. More than once I had been tempted to punch him. "Is it hard to get into America?"

"Sometimes. Sometimes not. Everyone has their own story. But it is always dangerous to cross the border.

"My first time, I was caught. *La migra* tied me up and threw me into a jail and left me until they had caught enough others to send us all back."

"*La migra?*"

"The border patrol. There is not just *la migra;* there are many other dangers. There are Mexican bandits. There are sex traffickers. My sister and others crossed the border. They were found by bandits. They raped some of the women and took everything they had, even their clothes. They were all made naked, then left in the desert.

"My sister was not raped because she was pregnant. They had to make their way across the desert without shoes or clothes or even water. There are much cactus and their feet were bleeding when they were found by *la migra.* They were happy to be found by *la migra.*" His expression darkened. "They are very lucky that they were *banditos* and not traffickers. I would not ever see my sister again."

"You said before that you have a wife."

"Yes. I have a wife."

"Where is she?"

"She is in Florida. She is a nanny for a rich family. She does not make much money, only a thousand dollars a month, but it is a much better life for her. She is in a house with air conditioning and good food. And the people she works for take her to the doctor if she is sick. They are helping her get papers. She is learning how to drive a car."

He nodded. "It is a much better life for her there. It is not safe for her with me because she is pretty. A pretty woman is not safe working the farms. One foreman had her work inside the building; then he tried to take her."

I frowned. "How often do you see her?"

"Once a year during the orange-picking season. That is when I go to Florida. I see her then for a week. We rent a hotel and make love and drink wine. The family she works for will sometimes make a gift for us. I wait all year for that week. Then I give her my money and she puts it in the bank. We are saving our money. Someday we will be together. Then we will have a baby. And she will have a better life." He looked up. "Do you have a wife?"

"I had one," I said.

Eddie frowned. "Did she die?"

"She divorced me."

He looked down. "Is that her ring you wear around your neck?"

"You noticed that."

"*Sí.* It is a nice ring."

"It was my wife's ring."

"Why did she leave you?"

"Because I cheated on her."

He frowned.

"I know. It was a long time ago."

"I am sorry."

"So am I." I looked at him. "That's why I'm walking. I'm walking to her. She lives in California."

"You are walking a *peregrinación,*" he said thoughtfully. "In the old days, they would walk for punishment. Sometimes they would even walk naked to show humility." He breathed out heavily. "That is a very hard walk, gringo."

"Your life is a very hard walk."

"Everyone has a hard walk," he said.

CHAPTER THIRTY-SIX

SOMETIMES PLANS, LIKE OUR OPINIONS, MUST BEND SO AS NOT TO BREAK.
— CHARLES JAMES'S DIARY

That night, as I lay in that moldy, lumpy bed, I thought about Eddie and his wife and how much he loved and sacrificed for her. Then I thought about my own wife. I had told myself that all my traveling and hard work was a sacrifice for her. But that was a lie. I had done it for my own glory. Or maybe for my fears. My greatest fear should have been losing her. How could I have let her go?

Next my thoughts turned to my grandfather and what he must have gone through and all he had suffered so I could live the life I had. My thoughts continued to my father as well.

I had always hated my father for his

cruelty, but my mother had once told me that his father had treated him as cruelly as he treated us. The victim became the aggressor. That's how it worked sometimes.

But I hated him for more than his cruelty; I hated him for his smallness. As I thought about that, it occurred to me, for the first time, that maybe that was what I should have respected him for most. His life *was* small. It had few payoffs, few downhill coasts, few — if any — moments of glory. It was all straight up the side of a rocky mountain to a barren peak, with nowhere to go from there. But he had dug in. He had made a foothold in this country, one that I was able to summit from. I had never given him credit for that. Not once.

As I thought about it, I realized that this was, perhaps, the true reason I had joined Eddie on the farm — to truly understand what had been done for me. And to start to forgive. True understanding often opens the door to forgiveness.

At that moment there was a breakthrough, in my heart as well as my mind. It was the first time I had thought about my father without hate or anger. In fact, it was the first time that I had thought about him with any measure of respect. It was a huge breakthrough. I had learned what I had come to Plainview for. It was time for me to get back to my trek.

I was still stuck without money. But as I considered my situation, I realized that there was a solution that wouldn't require my return to public: I could return to just one person. The one person whom I could trust my life on. I smiled at the thought. Amanda was going to have a complete mental meltdown. I was kind of looking forward to it.

The next day at lunch Eddie said to me, "What is wrong, gringo? You are very quiet today."

"Nothing is wrong," I said. "I'm just thinking."

He laughed. "Do not think too much. It will kill you."

"Probably." A few minutes later I asked, "What day is it today?"

"It is Friday, gringo."

"Friday," I repeated. "Friday is a good day to celebrate."

Eddie looked up at me. "Celebrate what?"

"My resurrection, Eddie. Tonight I'm taking you to Perlita's Taqueria to get some of that chili verde you told me about."

"You have gone *loco,*" Eddie said. "You have worked one week and you think you are rich now?"

I smiled. "I am rich, my friend. I'll arrange a ride to Perlita's with one of the truck drivers."

"You are *loco,* gringo."

"Maybe. So the question is, will you have dinner with a crazy man?"

He shook his head and grinned. "At Perlita's, I would be a crazy man not to."

CHAPTER THIRTY-SEVEN

**A TORTILLA WITH A FRIEND
IS GREATER THAN A FEAST
EATEN ALONE.
— CHARLES JAMES'S DIARY**

I made an arrangement with one of the farmhands to give us a ride to the restaurant. Eddie was quiet for most of the drive. I had noticed that he was usually quiet around the non-migrants, but I think tonight it was more. I think he was trying to figure out what I was doing.

Perlita's Taqueria looked like a warehouse because it had once been one. In its previous incarnation the building had been an industrial machine shop, and several remnants of its past remained in place like fossils — hulking, galvanized, and riveted contraptions that still leaked oil.

The floor was concrete and oil-stained, here and there covered with rugs. The walls were adorned with some of the worst artwork ever produced. It was so bad that it was actually borderline cool. Kitsch. There were black-velvet portraits of a mariachi band, bullet-belt wearing *banditos,* a busty Mexican beauty with a rose in her hair, and, of course, Elvis. An acrylic painting of the Virgin Mary hung above the cash register.

The restaurant's motif made me happy. I had learned long ago that when it comes to Mexican restaurants, the quality of the décor is inversely proportionate to the quality of the food. Based on that equation, Perlita's food was going to be remarkable.

Music was playing and the restaurant was almost full, its patrons mostly Hispanic. A young Mexican woman with a nose piercing and a rose tattoo on her neck greeted us as we walked in.

"Buenas noches, señorita," Eddie said.

"Buenas noches," she replied. "There are two of you?"

"Sí."

She grabbed two salsa-stained menus from the front counter and led us to a table beneath a painting of a gaucho at sunset.

I looked over the menu. "The chili verde is good?"

"It is all good, but the chili verde and the tamales are *muy bueno,"* he said, kissing his

258

fingers. He dropped his gaze to my pack, and his brow furrowed. "Gringo, why did you bring your backpack? You can trust our friends."

"I know. I just thought I'd keep it with me."

A moment later our waitress appeared. She was short, barely five feet and nearly as wide, with a pleasant face. She set a yellow plastic basket of tortilla chips in the middle of the table along with a small, colorful bowl of salsa.

"What may I get you gentlemen to drink?" She spoke without an accent.

"Agua, por favor," Eddie said.

"Do you have Bohemia?" I asked.

"No Bohemia," she replied. "We have Dos Equis and Corona."

"Two Dos Equis, please."

"Dos Dos Equis. Do you know what you would like to eat?"

I glanced at Eddie. "Have you decided?"

"Sí." He looked up at the waitress. *"Me gustaría el burrito de chile verde y un tamal de ají verde. Gracias."*

She turned to me. "And what will you have?"

"I'll have the same as my friend," I said. "And the cheese-stuffed jalapeños for an appetizer."

"Thank you," she said.

After she walked away, I turned back to Eddie. "Tell me about your wife."

He looked broadsided by the question. "Felicia," he finally said, speaking the name almost reverently. "She is my sweetheart."

"Where did you meet?"

"In our village. I am lucky she was born near me or I would not have found her."

"Does she like her work as a nanny?"

"Very much. But it makes her want to have another child. She would lose her job if she did. And I do not want to have a child I cannot see."

I thought about my own son. "I understand."

Twenty minutes later our waitress brought out large, steaming platters of food with the obligatory warning not to touch the plates. "Very hot," she said. *"Muy caliente."*

As Eddie had promised, the food was delicious. I hadn't had a large meal for more than a week, and my stomach hurt from my gluttony. For dessert I ordered a caramel flan followed by another beer for each of us.

It was nearly nine o'clock when our waitress brought out the check. I picked it up. Our meal was inexpensive, by my account, though not compared to the money I'd earned in the field. It was a lot of sweat and heartbeats for a meal.

Eddie looked concerned. "Is it much?"

"No," I said.

"I will help pay, *amigo.*"

I counted out cash to cover the bill. "I got it."

"It is not wise to spend all your money like this, gringo."

"It's the least I can do, my friend."

When we'd finished our beers, Eddie asked, "When are you ready to go back?"

I looked into his eyes. "I'm not going back, *amigo.*"

He looked at me quizzically. *"Qué?"*

"I brought you here to say good-bye. It's time for me to continue my walk."

Eddie still looked perplexed. "How will you do this with so little money?"

"I've got things figured out. In fact . . ." I reached into my pocket and pulled out a wad of money, the whole of my week's wages. I counted out fifteen twenty-dollar bills, three hundred of the five hundred forty dollars I had left and set it on the table in front of him.

Eddie just looked at me with surprise. "Gringo, what is this?"

"I want you to have it."

He looked even more confused. "Why are you giving me your money?"

"I don't need it," I said. "I'd give you all of it, but I need a little to get to where I'm going."

He just looked at the bills. "Gringo . . ."

"Take it, *amigo,*" I said.

He shook his head. "We all need money, gringo. What will you eat?"

"I ate enough tonight to last me a week."

Eddie didn't smile. He was clearly concerned that I had lost my mind.

"Look," I said. "I'm not *loco.* You don't need to worry about me. What you said yesterday, about other options, you were right. I just didn't see them." I pushed the bills closer to him. "Take it."

He still didn't take the money.

"Well, I'm not going to pick those back up, so you can take it with you or leave our waitress her biggest tip ever."

After a moment, Eddie took a deep breath, then reached out and took the bills, clutching them firmly. "Okay, gringo." As he looked up, his eyes welled with tears. "Thank you, *amigo.*"

"Thank you for helping me. You are a good man, Eddie. After I finish my walk, I would like to come back to see you. I'd like to help you get back with your wife. How will I find you?"

He shook his head. "You cannot find me.

There are millions of men like me. We are like drops of water in a river."

I thought for a moment. "Then you'll have to find me. I want you to do something. It's very important. *Muy importante.* Do you want to be with your wife?"

"Yes. Of course."

"Then you must do what I say." I took the waitress's pen and wrote down my email address on the back of my receipt. "This is very, *very* important. You must trust me. Do you have an email address?"

"Yes. It is how Felicia and I talk. But I have no computer. Sometimes I find an Internet café."

"Good. If it costs to use the Internet, pay for it. Use whatever money you have, but I want you to check your email. Not now, but in October or November, I want you to email me at this address. I want you to email me until you hear back from me. Will you do this?"

He nodded.

"Good. Now take this." I slid the paper over to him. "This is my email address. Do not lose it. Memorize it if you can. It is very, very important."

Eddie took the paper from me. "This is how I find you?"

"Yes. Do not lose this."

"I won't, *amigo.*" He touched his temple. "I have already put it in here. I have a very good memory."

"That's good," I said.

"Sometimes it is not good," he replied.

We stood. I grabbed my pack and we walked to the door. Near the front desk I had an idea. "I just thought of something. Do you know Felicia's address in Florida?"

"*Sí.* I know her address and her phone number."

"Excellent. Write it down for me." I grabbed a piece of note paper from the hostess station. "Just in case something happens."

Eddie wrote down the information. As he handed me the paper, he asked, "Why is this so important, gringo?"

"There's more to me than you know." I stowed the paper in a zippered pocket of my backpack. "I've arranged a ride for you back to the farm. I already paid him, so don't let him try to charge you again. Understand?"

"*Sí.* I understand, but where are you going?"

"To California."

We looked at each other for a moment and then embraced.

"*Adiós, hermano,*" Eddie said.

264

"Hasta luego," I replied. Then I turned and walked out the door. For the first time in many years, I felt like I had a true friend.

CHAPTER THIRTY-EIGHT

THERE ARE MOMENTS WHEN REALITY IS NOT ONLY STRANGER THAN FICTION BUT MORE ENTERTAINING AS WELL.
— CHARLES JAMES'S DIARY

I had made arrangements with a young farmhand named Keith to drive me to Amarillo and rent me a room at a cheap motel. I paid Keith for the motel and gave him a hundred dollars for his trouble.

After I took my things to my room, I walked next door to a Walgreens, where I purchased some strawberry Pop-Tarts, a bottle of milk, some travel-sized laundry detergent, a cheap can of shaving cream, a bag of disposable razors, and some hair gel.

For the first time in weeks, I washed my clothes; they turned the water in the bathtub a thick, muddy brown. Then I hung everything up to dry on the chipped metal railing

266

behind the motel and went to bed.

I woke stiff and tired the next morning. I think my body had finally let down from all the stress I'd been carrying, and I felt as though I'd passed through a nightmare of motorcycle gangs, crew leaders, and pigweed.

I got up, washed my face with cold water, then sat on the edge of the bed thinking about what I was about to do. I was about to let someone know that I was still alive. Once I did, there was no turning back.

Truthfully, there really wasn't much to think about. It wasn't what I had initially planned, but it's what circumstance (and a hairy motorcycle gang) had brought me to. I had twenty-two dollars and seventy-four cents left to my name. After that, my options were gone. I picked up the motel phone and dialed Amanda.

Amanda's phone rang six times before going to voice mail. I wasn't surprised that she didn't answer; I would have been more surprised if she had. For as long as I had known her, she had never taken a call from a phone number she didn't recognize. Ironically, one of the last things I said to Amanda at the airport curb was to watch for my call from an unknown number.

Fortunately, I knew the secret to getting

through. Persistence. I dialed her again. Again my call went to voice mail. I dialed a third time, then a fourth. On my fifth attempt she answered, sounding polite but exasperated. "This is Amanda."

It was so good to hear that voice. Surreal, but good. "Hi, Amanda," I said softly.

"Hi. Who is this?"

"It's Charles."

Pause. "Charles who?"

"Your friend Charles."

Nothing. I tried again. "It's me, Charles, your boss."

"This isn't funny. I'm hanging up."

"Amanda, I'm not dead."

"I'm hanging up."

She hung up. I groaned, then dialed her again. And again. Then again.

The third time, she answered, "Quit calling me!"

"You spelled *Beverly Hills* wrong."

There was a long pause. "What?"

"*Beverly Hills.* You spelled it wrong in the obituary. Don't you remember me mocking you about that in LA?"

Pause. "How do you know about that?"

"It's really me, Amanda. Ask me something that no one would know but me."

She hesitated for a moment, then asked, "Where were you when I called to ask if I could work for you?"

"I was in Birmingham, and you were in Des Moines. And you didn't call me, I called you. It was right after our Montgomery show, and I had just met Chris and Mila." There was a long, silent pause. "Amanda, I wasn't on the plane. I missed the flight."

There was another long pause. "What's your social security number?" Her voice was pitched with stress.

I rattled off the nine digits.

"This is freaking me out."

"Amanda, take a deep breath. Get centered."

"That's what you — he — always said."

"I knew this would freak you out. I also know that you're the only one I can trust. I need your help."

Suddenly her relief exploded into anger; she sounded like a frantic mother who had just found her lost child in a shopping mall. "I held a memorial service for you!"

"I know. I was there. I was the guy in the back row in the hat and sunglasses. You gave a beautiful eulogy. So did McKay. Laura's I could have done without."

"It *is* you." She started to cry. "Where have you been? Everyone thinks you're dead."

"I know. I want them to. I want everyone to think I'm dead but you."

"The business is shutting down. Everyone's gone."

"That's okay."

"It's not okay!" she erupted. "We built this together. And someone hacked into our business accounts and stole all the money!"

"No, they didn't."

"Yes, they did! You're not even . . ." She stopped. "It was you. You were hiding your money."

"I moved it to an offshore account. I wasn't about to let someone give it all away."

She broke down sobbing. After a while I asked, "Are you okay?"

"How could you do this to me?"

"I'm sorry. I didn't plan any of this. I left my backpack with all that money you gave me in an airport store. When I got off to get it, they closed the flight. I got lucky. I don't know why. Maybe it's God, maybe it's just dumb luck, but you know what a bad place I was in before I left. When this happened, I decided it was the universe telling me to figure things out."

"But what about *my* life?" she said. "I just started a new job."

"Quit it. You still work for me."

"Where are you?"

"Amarillo."

"Texas?"

"That's how far I've walked."

"Walked?"

"That's what I'm doing. Walking."

"You walked to Texas? How far is that?"

"Very far," I said. "I'm almost halfway."

"Halfway to where?"

"To LA. I'm walking Route 66."

She was speechless.

"I need your help to finish. I'm broke and I can't access my money. I need to borrow some."

"How much do you need?"

"I only need a few thousand to get by."

"Where should I wire it?"

"I'll have to figure that out. But first, I want you to call the Amarillo Marriott; it's downtown . . ."

"Just a minute, let me get a pen." I could hear her rooting around her desk. "All right."

"Where are you?" I asked.

"Home."

"You're still in Chicago?"

"For the time being. My new job may transfer me to New York."

"Quit it," I said again. "I want you to book me a room in the Amarillo Marriott."

"And if they're sold out?"

271

"It's Amarillo."

"Sorry. How many nights?"

"Two. No, make it three. I need some time to collect myself. I've been working the fields with the migrant workers and I'm pretty tired."

"Migrant workers? Charles, what's going on?"

"I'll put it in a book someday," I said. "Now, the money. I think our best bet is Western Union. They can give me cash."

"Just a minute, let me look them up." There was a short pause, then Amanda said, "There are three Western Union locations in Amarillo. One is just two blocks from the hotel. You'll need to give them the tracking number, my name, and the transfer amount. How much do you want?"

"Send me two thousand."

"Two thousand," she said, writing it down. "They'll also need a form of government-issued photo ID."

"I've got that. Wait, my ID is for Gonzales, not James. Make it out to Charles Gonzales. The same goes for the hotel room. I only have one ID."

"Good thing you thought of that," she said. "How do I get ahold of you? Do you still have your phone?"

"No. It got stolen. I need you to close it

down. Just call me at the hotel with the tracking number."

"Okay. Is there anything else I can do for you?"

"No. That's good for now. Remember, I don't want anyone to know I'm alive."

"I understand."

"Thank you, Amanda." I breathed out heavily. "You have no idea how good it is to talk to you."

"You have no idea how good it is to know you're alive. I still can't believe it." She was quiet a moment, then said, "I'm glad you're alive."

"Thank you, Amanda. Me too."

CHAPTER THIRTY-NINE

I HAVE FUTILELY CHASED HAPPINESS FOR SO LONG THAT I ALMOST DIDN'T RECOGNIZE IT WHEN IT SNUCK UP BEHIND ME.
— CHARLES JAMES'S DIARY

I gathered my things and walked the two miles to the Downtown Marriott. By the time I reached the hotel, Amanda had already booked my room — a nonsmoking king-sized suite on the concierge level. The woman behind the desk asked for my ID and a credit card for incidentals. I handed her my driver's license but told her I didn't have a card. She looked back at my account and apologized. "I'm sorry. It's all been taken care of."

Walking into the hotel was suddenly a new experience. Throughout my career I had stayed in hundreds of hotel rooms and taken them for granted. Now, after the migrant shack, everything looked different. It's no wonder my life had felt hollow for so long. I had stopped looking for beauty, then wondered why the world was so ugly. I had just turned on the television when the phone rang.

I picked it up. "Amanda?"

"Hi. I've got the tracking number."

There was a pen and notepad on the nightstand next to the phone. "Go ahead." She gave me the twelve-digit number. I wrote it down and thanked her.

"Now what?" she asked.

"I'm going to go get the money, then come back and get a massage."

"It sounds like you've earned it."

"Earned or not, I'll definitely appreciate it."

She hesitated a moment, then said, "Charles, you sound different."

"What do you mean?"

"You sound . . . lighter."

"What does that mean?"

She paused again. "I don't know. It's just good to have you back."

"Thanks again. For everything."

"No problem. Just don't go disappearing on me."

"I won't. Thank you."

"Talk to you soon. Bye."

I hung up. *Lighter?*

Everyone should have an Amanda — Amanda included. I called the hotel concierge and arranged for a massage. Then I walked over to the Western Union office and picked up the money. It felt good to be solvent again.

I went back to the hotel, ate a light lunch at the lobby restaurant, went back to my room, and took a nap.

I got up around four and went down to the hotel's spa. I relaxed for a while in the sauna and steam room, then went to my massage.

The masseuse reminded me a little of Monica. Her eyes. It was a pleasant fiction, lying there, pretending it was her touching my skin, rubbing my muscles. She used to rub my back every night when I'd get home from work.

I went back to my room and ordered dinner — halibut and scalloped potatoes, asparagus, and crème brûlée for dessert. As I was lying on my bed waiting for my meal, a thought hit me that I hadn't had in years. *I was happy.* I was actually happy. How long had it been? Here I was, away from everything I thought defined my life, only to find it.

At that moment it occurred to me that

happiness had come to me in the guise of gratitude. For the first time in as long as I could remember I was truly grateful for something — not fame or money or a fleeting splash in the media but seemingly small things made big through gratitude — a soft bed, cold water, food to eat.

For the first time I realized that gratitude and joy were connected, like conjoined twins. I couldn't be happy because I wasn't grateful and I wasn't grateful because I wasn't allowing myself to be. I was too busy hunting the next prize to appreciate the prize already at home. What I had was never enough, not because of the deficit in what I had but because of the deficit in me. And the cloud of my ingratitude obscured everything of value in my life: even something as precious as my Monica.

That's why I had lost her. I had stopped seeing the miracle of her. I had stopped realizing the blessing she was in my life. I had stopped being grateful for her. *She had stopped being my pearl.*

The epiphany seared my heart. If I was allowed a second chance, I would remind her every day how grateful I was to have her. More important, I would remind *myself* every day, and the rest would take care of itself.

As I pondered my newfound joy, my thoughts turned to Eddie. He would just be getting back from the fields about now, sitting down to a humble meal of warmed tortillas with mashed beans. A pang of guilt passed through me. He deserved the meal I was about to eat. If he were here, I would feed him. I hoped that I would have that chance. I hoped that he didn't forget to email me. I even prayed that he wouldn't. It was an awkward prayer, one of those, "I don't know if I'm talking to anyone or just the ceiling, but if you are there, please let me find Eddie so I can help him get back with his wife and have a good life."

I don't know if God hears those kinds of prayers, but if He is who people claim He is, I suspect He does.

CHAPTER FORTY

**CHALLENGES ARE LIKE
THUNDERSTORMS: WHERE
SOME SEE DARKNESS, OTHERS
FIND NOURISHMENT.
— CHARLES JAMES'S DIARY**

I slept in late the next morning. Really late.
Actually, it was afternoon when I finally
woke. The soft, full bed and its clean,
expensive linens felt luxurious. I ordered
eggs Benedict for lunch, with fresh-squeezed
orange juice and breakfast potatoes. Then I
showered and got dressed and went for a
walk. I know that might sound funny, but
walking was part of me now, and my mind
needed it as much as my body.

I walked about four miles to a downtown
mall and back. The city was warm and
windy and dry. I've heard Amarillo described as "a cow town on the edge of
metropolis," which seemed about right. I

279

had been to Amarillo twice before on one of my whirlwind seminar tours, but I had never really seen the place. I liked it this time. Maybe it wasn't what I had found in the city but in myself.

I went back to my hotel, turned on the television, and just zoned out for the next two hours. I was starting to think about dinner when there was a knock at my door. I opened the door without looking to see who was there.

It was Amanda. At first she just stared at me, her mouth agape. Then she threw her arms around me. "It really is you."

We hugged for at least a minute. When we parted, her cheeks were wet with tears. "I had to see you in person," she said. "I had to be sure it was you."

"You knew it was me."

"My head did," she said, "but my heart didn't."

"When did you get in?"

"Just an hour ago. I caught the first flight to Amarillo."

"I'm glad you came," I said. "Come in."

She had a carry-on bag, which she pulled into my room. Her eyes never left me, like she was afraid I might disappear again. After the door shut she said, "I still can't believe it. When I heard that the plane had crashed . . ." Her eyes welled up again. "So many things went through my mind. I blamed myself. If only I had put you on a different flight . . ."

"You can't blame yourself for something you had no control over."

"I can," she said. "I shouldn't, but I definitely can."

I smiled. "The truth is, you saved my life by making me go to that office birthday party."

"That party you hated," she said.

"The one I hated," I echoed. "I'm sorry." I looked her over. "Are you hungry?"

"Starved."

"Good. Let's go get some dinner."

Chapter Forty-One

**The Sojourn Has Changed,
but Not, I Think, As Much As
the Sojourner.
— Charles James's Diary**

At the concierge's recommendation, Amanda and I took a taxi to the Big Texan Steak Ranch. The restaurant is an Amarillo icon, a bright-yellow edifice with a half dozen Texas flags flying in front and a giant cowboy boot and steer in the parking lot. A sign on the steer advertised a free seventy-two-ounce steak, with the disclaimer *If eaten by one person in one hour.*

The restaurant was crowded, though from the size of the place, I suspected that it probably always was. We waited about a half hour for a table, then a waitress in a cowboy hat sat us at a table along one of the outer walls, which was about as much privacy as we were going to get. She brought us drinks served in red plastic cups in the shape of cowboy boots.

"I've never been here before," Amanda said.

"Neither have I. When was the last time we were in Amarillo?"

"It was two years ago. August."

I don't know how she did it, but Amanda never forgot a show or a venue.

After we had ordered, Amanda said, "You know the crash made international news. It's all anyone talked about for days."

"I know," I said. "I got to the point that I couldn't turn on the television."

She leaned forward to better hear me. "So tell me in detail how you missed the flight."

"Okay," I said, leaning forward myself. "You know we were cutting it close. And O'Hare was already chaos because of the weather, so by the time I got to the gate, I had missed the preboarding and there was a line that stretched to the end of the Jetway. You know how I hate waiting in lines, so I decided to go buy a phone charger."

"That's right," Amanda said. "Your phone was dead."

"I wasn't in a hurry, since the line was so long, but apparently the airline was, because when I got back to the gate, the line had somehow evaporated, and the gate agent was calling my name.

"I checked in. Then, halfway down the Jetway, I realized that I'd left my pack with my computer and all the money you gave me in the store where I'd bought the charger. So I hurried back out.

"By then the gate attendant was off helping other customers, so when I couldn't get her attention, I just ran to the store and got my pack. The girl in the store was slow as peanut butter, so by the time I got back to the gate, they had closed the Jetway door."

"Then why didn't the airline tell us you weren't on the flight?"

"Because the gate agent was overwhelmed with irate passengers, and when I finally got her attention, she told me to go to customer assistance, which was where I was still waiting when I learned the plane had crashed."

Amanda breathed out deeply. "It sounds like a complex conspiracy to keep you alive."

"Apparently."

"So why are you walking to California?"

"I ask myself that every day," I said. "You know what a mess I was in before I left. I just needed time to clear my mind.

"After the crash, it felt like the universe had given me a chance to rethink my life. I couldn't stay at home without being discovered, and I wasn't going to sit around in a hotel room. I knew it was only a matter of time before my passport was revoked, so I couldn't leave the country. So I decided to do what I always do when I'm stumped. I decided to walk."

"But why Route 66?"

"It chose me. Remember those nightmares I'd been having?"

"That's right," she said, nodding in remembrance.

"But I think it's more than that. As I thought over my life, I realized that the only time I had really been happy was back when I was with Monica. And not coincidentally, she's at the end of Route 66. Maybe it's a walk of penitence, but I think I've been headed back to her for a long time now, I just didn't know it.

"The universe had given me a second chance at life. I was hoping that maybe it would give me a second chance with Monica as well."

Amanda's expression abruptly fell. I knew the look on her face too well — the one she had whenever she had bad news she didn't want to tell me. My stomach instinctively knotted up. "What's wrong?" I asked.

Amanda shook her head. "I'm so sorry." She took a deep breath, then said, "Two days before your memorial service, Monica called to tell me she couldn't make it. She was really apologetic about it. She said that Gabriel had come down with strep and she didn't have anyone to watch him."

"Is he all right?"

"I'm sure he is," Amanda said. "That's not what I was going to tell you." She looked into my eyes. "I asked her how she was doing and she told me that she's getting married."

My chest froze.

"I'm really sorry," Amanda said again.

I didn't speak for a moment, then said angrily, "She sounds pretty broken up by my death."

"She was *very* upset," Amanda said. She reached over and touched my hand. "I'm so sorry."

Again I was speechless. Most of all I felt stupid. Why was I so surprised? Of course she was getting married. She was beautiful and smart and sweet. The real question was, Why hadn't she gotten married sooner?

Still, the news hit me in the gut like a sucker punch. It was several minutes before I could speak. I fought back the emotion that was crushing my chest and heart.

Amanda just looked at me sadly. After a while she said, "What are you going to do now?"

I slowly shook my head for a moment. Then I said, "I'm going to do what I always do. I'm going to finish what I started."

"You're going to finish walking the Route?"

"Yes."

"Are you going to see Monica?"

"Yes."

"And after that?"

I looked her in the eyes and said, "I'll let you know when I get there."

The next morning, Amanda and I went to a mall phone store and got me a simple flip phone so she could reach me in case of an emergency. She also gave me one of her credit cards, saying that she would add me to the account and send me my own card as soon as it came to her.

Amanda flew back to Chicago that afternoon. The last thing she said to me before getting into a taxi was, "You really have changed, Charles."

I asked, "Is that a good thing?"

She replied, "What do you think?"

"I think that's a safe answer," I said.

She smiled, then said, "You seem more at peace."

"I'll take peace," I said.

I shut the door, and the taxi headed off

for the airport. The next day I started back out on the road.

EPILOGUE

My therapist, Dr. Fordham, once said to me, "The reason we start something is rarely the reason we continue doing it." Perhaps that's true with diets and habits, but I found it true for me in walking as well. I still intended to see Monica. I owed her that. Maybe I would even congratulate her on her upcoming nuptials. She deserved to be happy. She deserved to be loved. She deserved better than I had given her. She deserved to be someone's pearl. I wanted her to know that. I wanted her to hear that from my own mouth.

And I wanted to meet my son. I didn't know what I would say to him. What do you say to someone you've so utterly failed? I didn't even know if he knew I existed — or that I had supposedly died. How confusing this would be for him. For the first time I thought it might be better if he didn't know that I was still alive.

What I did know was that Monica would protect him. She was fiercely protective of those she loved. That had once included me.

I didn't know what I would say when I reached her, but I still had three states and twelve hundred miles to figure that out. That's a lot of miles. A lot of steps. And a lot of time to think. I would figure something out by then. In the meantime, all I knew for certain was that it was time to return to my walk.

ACKNOWLEDGMENTS

I would like to thank my editor, Christine Pride, for her patience, as well as the rest of my Simon & Schuster family: Jonathan Karp, Carolyn Reidy, Richard Rhorer, Sarah Reidy, Elizabeth Breeden, and Benjamin Holmes. Thanks, always, to my agent, Laurie Liss, for running interference.

The doctor Charles meets in Joplin is partially based on a friend and a man I admire, Dr. George Ritchie, who has since passed away. His book *Return from Tomorrow* helped lead me back to God. I highly recommend it.

To my wife, Keri: You are love and light. Thank you for your example.

ABOUT THE AUTHOR

Richard Paul Evans is the #1 bestselling author of *The Christmas Box*. Each of his more than thirty novels has been a *New York Times* bestseller. There are more than thirty million copies of his books in print worldwide, translated into more than twenty-four languages. He is the recipient of numerous awards, including the American Mothers Book Award, the *Romantic Times* Best Women's Novel of the Year Award, the German Audience Gold Award for Romance, two Religion Communicators Council Wilbur Awards, the *Washington Times* Humanitarian of the Century Award and the Volunteers of America National Empathy Award. He lives in Salt Lake City, Utah, with his wife, Keri, and their five children. You can learn more about Richard on Facebook at Facebook.com/RPEFans, or visit his website, RichardPaulEvans.com.